DECODED

The Luciferians are superrich, they are flashy and they are powerful. This is the new face of devil worship in Nairobi. Christians are warned to be on guard. The slightest slippage may lead to eternal damnation!

DECODED

The Luciferians are superrich, they are flashy and they are powerful. This is the new face of devil worship in Nairobi. Christians are warned to be on guard. The slightest slippage may lead to eternal damnation!

Sam Okello

Published by Sahel Publishing Association, a subsidiary of Sahel
Books Inc
P.O. Box 18007
00100
Nairobi, Kenya
www.sahelpublishing.net

A Sahel Book

Interior Design: Hellen Wahonya Okello
Cover Design: Hellen Wahonya Okello
Printed in India, UK, U.S.A

To you, the pilgrim

PROLOGUE

When Randy stumbled on the second secret he felt his head spin. Not too long ago he had sneaked into his wife's purse and pulled out her cell phone. He had been married to Kate for twenty years. They were not young in age or in the game of marriage. For those who knew how close they were as a couple, they were the duo to emulate. They had even heard that parents in their church lifted them up as an example to sons and daughters who looked for a life partner. They had so much love between them that friends and family feared one would never live without the other. What nobody knew was that beneath that veneer of calm there was now simmering tension since Randy had purposely pried into Kate's Gucci handbag and pulled out her Nokia cell phone. Her forty days were up!

Randy had not intended to pry, but the previous night Kate's phone had rung like seven times, by his count, and each time it had she had walked into the bathroom and locked herself in to talk. The talk was nothing more than endless giggles and girl chat—which puzzled him. He couldn't understand why Kate would want to get into the bathroom to talk. It just wasn't like her. Something had to be going on. But what was it? That's what he was going to find out tonight. This was urgent.

Waiting until Kate got into the shower and he heard the steady gush of water off the showerhead, he tiptoed into the bedroom and went straight for the bag. It was perched on the dresser, where Kate had carelessly flung it when she got home from her well-paying job at the Safari View Towers, in Upper Hill. It may have been as a result of daily routine that she found it okay to hurl things on the dresser; after all, Randy had never done anything as silly as being nosy and wasn't about to suddenly start a crazy habit, right?

As the soft caress of the shower took its toll and Kate started to enjoy herself, Randy locked his finger and thumb around the ring that hid the phone and gently pulled it back. It didn't take long before he had the shiny black gadget. Fitted with all the features a modern gizmo could afford, it took him time to figure out how to operate it; but he eventually did. Within seconds, he was right on with the racy texts that had been exchanged between Kate and Vivian.

His finger trembling, Randy hit the button to Inbox and read the first message:

> *Last night was so special. I will replay it in my mind for years. I love you!*

Randy's jaw dropped. What? Who had written to Kate this stuff? No. This couldn't be a woman. This was Kate's boyfriend. The two cheats were just using the name Vivian to hide an ongoing affair. But why in the world would Kate get into an affair? Hadn't he bought her everything? She had a silver BMW, a sprawling bungalow in Runda and two houses in Milimani, Kisumu. She also had a handsome son who protected her like a special gift; and if everything went according to plan, they were on target to host a throbbing twentieth anniversary, surrounded by friends and family...in Watamu. Why was Kate doing this?

He hit the next text.

> *I love the way you kiss me. I wish Randy could kiss me just the way you do it!*

This time Randy's jaw didn't drop. He looked at the phone to be sure it was indeed Kate's phone he had in his hand. Kate's phone was fitted with a camera which boasted a feature that ensured its images sharpened to a resolution above 300 DPI. It also came with Internet capability and other trendy features that made it vastly superior to the Motorola he had. Wherever Kate went, people always marveled at her phone. It was special in every way. Determining it was Kate's indeed, Randy dropped on the bed and squeezed the forming tears. There was no need to read anymore. Two racy texts were enough to tell the story.

Fuming, he fell back on the bed and waited for Kate to get back from her shower. No need to attack a woman who was clearly having a time of her life under the lulling spray of the gentle showerhead. Minutes later, Kate breezed in with a Dolly Parton tune on her lips and a smile sweet enough to melt the ice on Mt Kenya. She was in a jovial mood; hoped to have a romantic night with her husband.

But Randy was not in the mood tonight. The last thing on his mind right now was romance. And even though he was going to be gentle about the whole thing, he didn't want to act in a manner that made Kate think he would ever condone such behavior.

"Why, Kate?" There was deep pain in his eyes.

Kate's breath caught. "What's the matter?"

"The texts!"

The texts? My God! The bright smile, so radiant only seconds ago, instantly vanished from her thin lips. *He has found out? So he has been sneaking and reading my text messages? How dare he?*

"What is it I have not done that you have to find another man to do for you, sweetheart?"

Kate looked down, feeling awful about hurting Randy. He had been too nice over the years to deserve this kind of callous treatment. But she also reasoned that there was nothing wrong with having a thing with another woman. It wasn't like she was sleeping with a man behind his back. A woman just wasn't a big deal.

"What's going on, Kate? Who is this guy?"

Kate drew a deep breath, then dropped in next to Randy. She had to decide how she handled this matter without causing too much conflict in the home. But boy, was it really wise to talk about Vivian and her lesbianism now? Was it okay to break Randy's heart by declaring she had been in love with Vivian and that the whole matter was beyond their control because it was in the hands of the ancient dragon?

"Talk, sweetheart…?"

Kate took Randy's hand and gave it a gentle rub. Noting that he didn't resist, she wiped a forming tear off the corner of her eye and said, "I'm so sorry, Randy."

Randy shrugged. "About what?"

"The texts."

"Fine. But who is the guy?"

Kate exhaled in a staggered fashion, then decided she was going to release her information in bits and pieces until Randy weaved the tale by himself. The first was this. "It's not a guy, sweetheart."

In Randy, there was no immediate reaction, but looking at his wife with that characteristic plain colorlessness, he said, "What's that supposed to mean, Kate? You a lesbian now?"

A lesbian? That word didn't sound right. Lesbians were societal deviants, girls who did bad things on other girls. In fact, hadn't Pastor Ogwoka, of the Remnant Church, preached against that practice more than once and connected it to the great controversy between God and Satan? Hadn't he called sex—in all its deviant forms—a weapon in the hands of Luciferian agents? No, Kate wasn't a lesbian at all; she wasn't even a Luciferian, she was just in love with Viv. That was it!

"You are seeing a woman?" Randy pressed.

Instead of answering, this time Kate dissolved into tears and rested her head on Randy's shoulder. Something told her to lie lie lie. But unwilling to keep the truth from her man any longer, she finally broke down and said, "Sweetheart, it is a long story. It started the night I told you I was to attend a meeting in Mombasa."

Randy didn't say a thing.

"I went to Mombasa okay, and I did what I went there to do, but that's also where my fling with Viv started."

"Interesting. Let me ask you this then—other than she being your secretary, who really is she?"

Kate looked down to avoid the penetrating eyes. Randy had his eyes on her, his breath slow by her side, his body temperature just right; not as if he was seething or anything. If he was mad at all, Kate was unable to detect it right now. She had never seen him so controlled when mad. This felt strange. But what did she really know about Vivian? Not much. So rather than talk, she settled on a shrug for now.

"Are you sure it's not a man we are dealing with here?" Randy asked, this time sounding like it was Kate's last chance or else...

Kate shook her head. No, it wasn't a man for sure. But wait—did it make it any better that it wasn't a man? Deciding there was no way to sanitize this situation, she brought her eyes up slowly, met Randy's gentle eyes and lingered, then slowly turning away, she said, "Vivian is my *gal* at the office. That's all I know about her."

"Your gal?"

"That's what I call her."

"Is that another way of saying you and her are lov…?"

"It is," Kate said quickly to avoid hearing the word *lovers*, which Randy was about to let fly off his lips.

But what followed was even more stinging. He said, "Are you sleeping with your secretary?"

"I'm so sorry, Randy!"

I take that as a yes. Randy took a second to absorb the news. It was too much for one evening. Deciding he'd heard enough for now, he left Kate in the bedroom and hobbled to the veranda to catch a breath of fresh air. It was while he stood out there—his eyes on the chirping weaverbirds on the thorn trees in the yard—that Kate followed him and delivered her final, stinging salvo.

She wasn't a *Slut for Satan* just yet, but she was a closet Luciferian!

ONE

Vivian was a towering, slender woman from Kendu-Bay, a tiny town in Western Kenya with a reputation that didn't match its size. Born into the large family of a respected civil servant in the Kenyan government, Viv had gone to schools in and around the city of Kisumu, winding down her studies at a secretarial training institute in Nairobi. A last born in a family of six grown girls, she grew up among rowdy boys in her village and picked up tendencies that made her more comfortable in the company of men than women. For the most part, Vivian saw herself more as a man than a woman. She felt strong and driven in ways that made her curve a niche as the leader of a new breed of village girl—*the rumbling tomboy.*

In most rural African homes, tradition ruled the day. Whereas women were expected to go to the *shamba* and help Mama with the multiplicity of chores at home, Vivian wanted to do the man-thing. She always pleaded with Mama to let her go out to the grazing fields with the boys. She enjoyed talking crap with boys, shooting weaverbirds and sparrows off the euphorbia and jacaranda branches, and whistling along as the boys led the cows, goats and sheep to the pond to quench their thirst. That was vintage Viv.

Then, eventually seeing no harm in wearing certain forms of clothing that were easily identifiable as men's, she started wearing tight male denims, faded Chicago Bulls T-shirts and a string of ill-fitting Dallas Cowboys caps that she shoved in backwards. It was all in an effort to fit in with a group of rustic boys who, though they lived in the village, felt kind of trendy and wanted to identify with the dazzling screen characters they watched in the action-packed Western thrillers and in glamorous professional athletics.

Through her days in primary school, Vivian kept up the trend of hanging out with the boys. At class, during breaks and at lunch time, she actively sought the company of boys; at times being the most vocal of all and spewing the loudest string of outrageous epithets. There were times concerned teachers called her aside and scolded her, but she just couldn't help it; matter of fact, she saw absolutely nothing wrong with the way she conducted herself. To her, it was normal.

But one Sunday afternoon, after attending a refreshing service at the Pentecostal Church just down the bend, she had come home with two friends and was about to leave for the market for an evening stroll when Mama called her back. "I need to talk to you," Mama said in a rather flat, unflattering tone. "Would you give me a minute of your time?"

"Not now, Mama," Vivian shot back.

"Now it is!"

Vivian stopped and looked at Mama quizzically. What was the matter with her? But she didn't want to ask questions. She detected that beneath that veneer of calm was consuming fury; what she didn't know was what had caused it. She didn't have to wait long to find out, though, because as soon as she stepped back into the house, Mama's tongue let it eject like a fusillade. "Don't you have female friends, Vivian?"

Taken aback by the sudden hostility, Vivian never answered; she started crying, then limped into the dimly-lit corridor and on to her room. The room was not large by any measure and slept awkwardly adjacent to Mama's. Its walls were cream, which made it feel larger than it really was, and it boasted one sizable window, which overlooked a thicket and a seasonal pond yonder. There were pictures of Vivian and her friends, and a few of her with other family members, on the wall.

The floor of the bedroom, just like that in the rest of the house, was plain cement, except in the narrow portion where Vivian spread a fluffy carpet to avoid contact with the night-long cold when she woke up in the morning. At the corner Vivian had a movable dresser where she kept all the clothes Mama had bought her but she rarely wore.

It was while she still cried in there, stunned by the sudden turn of events, that icy-eyed Mama pried the door open and walked stiffly in like a seasoned NYPD detective. With characteristic gusto, and not in the least apologetic about the embarrassment she had just caused Viv, she said, "I just chased away your good-for-nothing friends!"

Vivian's breath caught and she wiped her tears. "What! Why did you do that, Mama?"

"How long did you expect them to wait at the gate for you while you cried? Or did you want me to entertain them for you?"

Vivian jumped off the springy bed and shoved her little feet into the pair of slippers bathed in clay dust. But just as she was about to dash off, Mama grabbed her by the hand and told her to sit down.

"What's wrong, Mama? What have I done?"

Mama dropped onto the bed, right next to Vivian, then drew a deep breath before talking. "Look, Vivian, I know it's not fair of me to erupt so suddenly like this, but something just got into me. I don't know what it is, but it did." She let that sink in, then she plodded on like her words had acid in them. "I've been hearing some of the craziest rumors about you and the boys!"

"What rumors?" Vivian asked defensively.

"Rumors that you have boyfriends; that you are always in the company of boys and may even be sleeping with them."

"You mean Ken and Kevin?"

Mama didn't know and didn't care; what she cared about was that Vivian change her ways. But aware she had come out a bit too strong and may have ambushed a girl with no ill intentions at all, she just as abruptly mellowed and said, "Listen, my dear girl, most villages are tough places; ours is even tougher. Girls who go around with boys are soon branded names and may never find men to marry them."

"But, Mama, Ken and Kevin are just friends!"

"But why them?" Mama asked. "Why not have female friends?"

"But women gossip too much, Mama."

"Really?"

"They're so fussy!"

"About what?"

"Every last thing," Vivian said. And in that moment she turned slowly to seek out Mama's eyes. When she found them and their eyes locked, she added, "Girls talk ill of others, Mama. I bet you heard those silly rumors about me from them girls, right?"

But avoiding to confirm or deny the source of the damaging rumors, Mama followed up with a quick question. "Are you dating any of those two boys?"

"No!"

"Are they trying to date you?"

Vivian thought for a second, then she exhaled in a staggered fashion, but she didn't talk.

"What should I make of that silence?" Mama asked.

"I don't know."

"Then listen to me," Mama said. Her voice was stern, but her face retained what Vivian felt was deceptive calm. "Boys are after only one thing—they eventually want to sleep with you!"

"Mom!"

"It's true, Vivian. It may take a week, a month or ten years, but if you befriend a boy today, one day he'll want to sleep with you. We don't call them dogs for nothing."

"And Dad?"

"What about him?" Mama asked sharply. If Vivian's intention was to unsettle the elderly lady, the plan had just succeeded beautifully, because even though the man had been dead for years, villagers had never given his parted soul a break. Stories about his philandering ways still did the rounds with a frequency that stunned just about everybody. There were men who were known to use him as justification for their waywardness when they were caught cheating. They asked their wives to be nice—just like Vivian's *mama* was.

"Was Dad a dog, Mama?" Vivian pressed, her tone laced with a bit of hurt, a bit of inquisitiveness, a bit of...something chocking!

But unwilling to go down that road, Mama took Vivian's hand and stood up. "Your father has been dead for years, Vivian. Do you really think it's fair to discuss him that adversely when he's not here to defend himself?"

"Meaning he was a do...?"

"Let's talk later," Mama said and started to walk out. As she shut the door behind her, she said, "Vivian, I'm just looking out for you."

"I know, Mama, but they are lying about me and they are lying about Dad. Dad was not what you just called him."

Mama felt a crash of pain on her chest, but pressed on. Vivian was too young to discuss her father with; maybe someday she was going to tell her about the man; how sleazy he was; the lack of self-control; how he never saw a lady he didn't want to go after.

But when would that day come?

———

After Vivian's mom left her room, she felt so mad and so lonely. Why was her own mom willing to believe the crap from some jealous, silly girls and not her? Was it wrong to have male friends? Was it wrong to want to do men things? Distressed about the situation, she collapsed onto her bed and allowed herself space to think about issues. It wasn't until around 9:30 p.m. that she got off the bed and walked straight into the living room, where Mama was now knitting. Looking her in the eye, she said, "Mama, I've given what you told me careful thought. I've come to the conclusion that I will never let what people say dictate the pace and direction of my life."

"That works well when you are right," Mama said, looking up to find her eyes. "When you are wrong it is a killer philosophy."

"I know I'm right."

Mama set the items on her hand on the dark coffee table and got up. She walked toward Vivian, a thought on her mind, then stopped just before reaching her. Talking in a softer tone this time, she said, "Vivian, let's never talk about your father again, okay?"

Vivian drew a deep breath and wanted to say something, but she held herself in check.

"Look, I don't want to talk about the women your father ran around with; that still hurts me," Mama said.

"But Dad was a good man," Vivian protested.

"He was a bad man!"

A bad man? Vivian jumped from her living room loveseat and wiped the sweat on her face. This was the year 2015. And this was Nairobi. Why were things that happened in her life so many years ago still having resonance in her life today? She had thought that once she moved to Nairobi her life in the village would slowly fade, give way to a brand new life, full of new thoughts, but nothing seemed to have changed; if anything she had gone from loving men to loving women and now to loving both.

Could Kate's insightful pastor have been right about *Sluts for Satan?* Was he on to something about sex and the great controversy?

Pastor Ogwoka was a man to watch!

Two

Randy couldn't believe his ears. He had known Vivian as the pretty girl who smiled warmly with him whenever he visited Kate at the Safari View Towers, in Upper Hill. Brought up in a deeply Christian home, he could have never guessed that the dashing beauty behind the desk on 8th floor was a lesbian. How could she be? Hadn't he seen a string of men come to that office ostensibly for official reasons only to end up chatting, winking and melting at her infectious smile? Hadn't she, once or even twice, made comments that he had interpreted as invitation to start a thing with her? How could a woman like that have no interest in men?

Confused by what Kate had just told him, he decided he needed to take an evening walk. He wanted to think things through; to weigh the implications of what his wife of more than twenty years had just told him. Being a cold evening, he kissed Kate's cheek and wore his tweed jacket, then he said he would be right back.

"No, Randy," Kate said alarmed, fearful that Randy was too hurt to be left alone. "I'm coming with you."

"No, Kate. It's better that I be alone for a while."

"Then tell me where you are going."

Randy hesitated, looked his wife in the eye, then he said, as he straightened his tweed jacket, "Just taking a walk, hon. I'll be back."

"Let me come?"

Randy shook his head and it hurt him to see Kate wince, but it had to be this way. He needed time to think. For twenty years plus he had lived with Kate and had come to a point in his life where he believed surprises were behind them. At forty three, he thought he could never do anything irrational to jeopardize the stability of his marriage; and he believed Kate was also mature enough to do whatever it took to keep the sweet glow of romance alive between them. So what was this sudden news about loving Vivian? And just how could he have missed the signs this long?

Drawing a deep breath, Randy forced a dry kiss on Kate's cheek then, without another word, he walked down the corridor, into the living room, then he was gone.

The minute Randy slammed the door behind him, Kate dashed to the window with tears in her eyes, watched as he slowly faded into the dusk of a cloudy evening, then picked up her cell phone and dialed.

On a second ring, Vivian looked at the caller ID and answered. "What's up, sweetheart?"

"Not good!"

"Not good? What's the matter?"

"The matter is…Randy knows about you and I."

It was like a dagger to the heart. Vivian couldn't believe this day had finally come. For more than a year now, she had worried that one day Randy would find out about them and he was going to be mightily pissed. Hoping to minimize the damage when that day came, she had rehearsed with Kate what to say and how to cover things up.

"But that will depend on how and what he'll have found out," Kate had warned a cocky Vivian.

"That's true," Vivian had said. "But I assure you, whatever he finds out all you'll have to do is say that things are not what they seem to be."

"And that will fool him?"

"No," Vivian had said. "It'll buy you time; give you a chance to reach me for a plan of action."

Well, that day had come and now Kate was on the line with the last thing she'd expected to hear today. Just hours ago, in town, Kate and Vivian had gone to Manhattan Hotel and had what they always called the Luo dish. For them, the Luo dish meant fried chicken with *ugali* and traditional greens. The greens were normally *osuga* or *apoth*. To enjoy the meal, they washed their hands and took the chicken piece by hand. After each bite, they followed with a golf-ball size of *ugali*. Just by watching them eat, it was easy to tell they enjoyed the Luo dish.

After the Manhattan meal Kate and Vivian had gone back to the office through Kenyatta Avenue, then into Uhuru Park. That park, once a den of thieves and home to thugs, had been vastly improved by the Kibaki government, working in conjunction with the newly-elected administration at City Hall. Unlike its former self, the park now boasted beautiful flowers, improved toilets and newer paved paths. On Sundays, when most lower class Nairobians visited to enjoy horse-riding, boat rides, and young lovers came to enjoy the beautiful sunshine Nairobi's blue skies regularly opened up to offer, a growing list of televangelists also rented the grounds to conduct well-attended services from which they raised thousands of shillings.

At the office, Kate and Vivian had found their colleagues out for field duty and had gone into Kate's office to make up. For nearly thirty minutes they touched, kissed and giggled. So much fun. But that was in the afternoon. This evening that rendezvous felt like it had happened many years ago. Things were not good!

"Gal, did you hear me?" Kate asked, surprised by Vivian's long silence.

Vivian exhaled in a staggered fashion, then she said, "Where is Randy and where are you?"

"I'm in the bedroom and Randy has just stormed out," Kate said. "He is pissed and looks like a buffalo about to charge!"

"Okay, let's go over this slowly. How did he find out?"

Willing herself, Kate walked Vivian through the evening, telling her in vivid detail how Randy's shock pained her; how she'd decided to come clean; how he'd stormed out of the house; how he was out there in the streets taking a walk alone. "Can it get any worse than this, gal?" she finally asked, groaning in a low hum like a wounded lioness.

"You shouldn't have talked," Vivian said.

"I shouldn't have talked? He's my husband, hello—!"

"So what?"

Kate felt hurt. What was Vivian saying? That it didn't matter how Randy felt? Didn't she know Randy had been her sweetheart over the years? And didn't she know that in spite of the blossoming love between them Randy was still the one she really loved and cared for? How could she treat Randy with such disdain?

"Ok, gal, that didn't come out well at all," Vivian said. "Let me rephrase my statement."

"Doesn't matter, Viv. Don't bother. For the first time I know how you really regard my husband," Kate said, bitterness raw in her cracking voice. "Makes me wonder whether this has been your game plan all along?"

"You mean breaking you up?"

"Yes, Viv. Has it?"

Vivian wanted to deny it, but she quickly thought of the time, almost six months ago, when she had lured Kate to a

Japanese restaurant in Westlands on a Saturday afternoon and had asked Kate to marry her. She recalled how stunned Kate had seemed and how she had quickly steered talk away from the subject of marriage the rest of the evening. The following Sunday Vivian had revisited the subject, this time confronting Kate with concrete proposals about how they were going to find an apartment in Kileleshwa and live together without having to worry about the stares and whispers of gossipers.

"How about Bill, my little boy?" Kate had asked.

"He'll adjust; he ain't that little no more," Vivian had said softly and persuasively. "Even Randy will adjust sooner than you think. He'll just find another girl and off they'll sail into midlife bliss together!"

"Huh! Are you kidding me?"

Scared stiff by the prospect of watching Randy sail away with another girl, Kate had firmly protested Vivian's plans. She had said, "Look, Vivian, I love and care for you, but I can't leave Randy. I love Randy too much, and I love Bill too much to want to ruin our home. We can love each other without having to alter anything around us." And that's how that evening had ended in a huff.

"Vivian?"

"Sorry, gal, I got distracted again," Vivian deadpanned. "As I was saying, breaking you up was never my plan; I just wanted you and I to love each other. I wanted you to realize that your future was with me, not with Randy and Bill."

"So you wanted Randy and I separated?"

"Not separated, divorced," Vivian said bluntly.

Kate was taken aback by Vivian's cold declaration. How could she be such a stone?

"Better still," Vivian added coldly, "I wanted Randy permanently kept away from you!"

"Barred by law you mean?"

"Yes!"

"As in kept away from me like he was a stalker?"

"By any means possible!"

Kate looked at the phone and cursed into it. She followed the curse with a string of epithets, until she heard Vivian laugh out loud.

"You can laugh now, you evil woman," Kate screamed, "but I'll have the last laugh!"

Vivian hung up. *I don't talk to delirious idiots.* In her mind's eye she could see Kate in her South C bedroom, probably hiding from Randy and Bill, completely screwing up this situation by behaving as if it was the end of the world. It was just so annoying.

———

South C *was* a middle-income estate located just minutes from Nairobi's Central Business District, tucked in the western corner of the rapidly expanding metropolis. Covering an area that spread from Nyayo Stadium and pushed back to embrace Nairobi West and a conflagration of gated communities like Akiba, Mugoya and others, the estate was accessed through Uhuru Highway to the west, Langata Road to the south and Jogoo Road to the deep east. Within that estate was the latest gated community to spring up called Spring View. It was in that community that Randy, Kate and Bill lived.

This evening, when Randy stormed out of the house, he took the stretch that brought him toward the gate. That stretch, fortified with bumps to slow vehicles down because of kids playing, was also lined with beautiful African roses and a few other exotic varieties. Because of the relative newness of the houses, the stretch was clean and the general area very attractive. From talking to neighbors, Randy had come to realize that most people who lived at Spring View were career civil servants, seasoned lawyers and doctors—and some of Nairobi's thriving businessmen and women.

Randy reached the manned iron gate and turned left toward the Nairobi Institute of Water Management, an institution that stood just minutes away from home. As he walked slowly in that direction, he thought about what Kate had just told him, how it had come out like a dagger to the heart. He couldn't believe it even now. His wife was a lesbian? A possible Satanist? What had gone wrong?

"Dad?"

Bill's voice stunned Randy and he turned instantly. What was the boy doing here this late in the evening?

"Dad, Mama told me to take a walk with you!"

Randy took the boy's hand and managed a thin smile. "What's Mama cooking?" he asked.

"She's not cooking," Bill said.

"Oh really? Then what is she doing?"

Bill looked at his dad, then looked down. He wanted to tell his dad the truth, but he feared Dad would think he was the reason Mama was crying, so he said instead, "Daddy, do you know Aunty Vivian?"

THREE

Bill was the only son of Randy and Kate. Born nearly two years after the celebratory wedding officiated by Pastor Chesimet, he was tall, dark and super-athletic. His eyes were bright, just like his mother's, and his manner favored more the folks on his mother's side of the family than his father's. He liked dressing casually, always having endless arguments with his dad, who saw life and success through the prism of spiffy jackets, silk ties and stripped blue suits. With his long legs and quick arms, he enjoyed playing basketball, a popular multi-billion dollar sport he picked up when Randy and Kate lived in the United States.

A good friend of his mom's, Bill was always protective of Kate's feelings. He was perpetually on guard whenever Mama was home, working hard to keep her from getting hurt in any way. Whenever arguments erupted between his two opinionated parents, he instinctively took Mama's side even though when calm was restored he would concede to his dad Mama was wrong!

Tonight Bill had done something he had never done before, though. He had followed Dad down the street and asked an unusual question—even though he had tried to slip it in as a by the way.

Dad, unsure why Bill had asked the question, said, "I've talked to Vivian a couple of times, son, but I don't really know her that well. Why did you ask?"

It was turning dark and the streetlights had just been turned on. Nairobians who lived within the gated communities of South C were returning home from work and businesses that took them to various destinations across the sprawling city. At this hour, the streets were packed with the latest model cars from Japan and Europe; and even though Toyota claimed that *Every car in front is always a Toyota*, there were other brands that were neither Japanese nor European; they were American. Judging by the sheer number of cars on the streets of South C, it was evident that Nairobi was a fast-emerging city in Africa.

The economy of the thriving city—just like that of the rest of the country—was clearly on an upward swing. Regional organizations and global multinationals based their operations in Nairobi. Add to that the influx of refugees from neighboring hotspots like Somalia and southern Sudan and what you had was a city crowding fast and was awash in cash. The only fear that seemed to hold the otherwise vibrant city captive was the unpredictability of politics.

And that fear wasn't unfounded. Just a couple of years ago, the country was nearly thrown to the gods when unprecedented violence erupted after disputed elections. Since then, Kenyans—Nairobians in particular—had watched each crested political wave with wariness, wondering which great wave would sweep the tenuous gains a coalition government had put together into the deep seas. And now, after years of watching the swelling number of Somalis with trepidation, there was a rising xenophobic tide against them; and by extension the Moslems. This unwarranted xenophobia had caused a situation where opinion leaders had sounded the alarm, warning that within twenty years there would be a confrontation between the Moslems and the Christians.

"Dad?"

"Yes, Bill."

Bill shrugged, then said, "I asked you a question."

"No, I asked you a question," Dad shot back.

"Ok, ok, so you want to know why I asked about Aunty Vivian?"

Dad nodded. "Sure."

"It's because I heard Mama talk to her before she started crying." He exhaled sharply. "Dad, they were arguing!"

"Really? About what?"

Bill didn't answer right away. He wasn't doing this to hurt his mom, he just wanted Aunty Vivian confronted so she could leave Mama alone.

"Bill, did you hear what they were arguing about?" Dad pressed.

"Yes, Dad."

"What?"

"A marriage or something like that."

Randy stopped and drew a deep breath. "Marriage?"

"Yes, Dad."

"Who was to marry who?"

Bill looked his dad in the eye and saw the pain and the shock. Clearly something even worse than he'd feared was going on here. He should have listened more carefully to what Mama and Aunty Vivian were saying, that way he'd have known who was to marry who; now he didn't and it scared him.

"Look, Bill," Dad said, noting his confusion. "I'll talk to Mama about this. Don't worry about anything. How was school today?"

Bill was a student at a British school in Lavington. He was bright and well loved by his teachers and classmates. Having returned to Kenya from the United States, where he was already used to the American system of quizzes and semester exams, the Kenyan system where one giant exam was done in class eight spooked him. Stunned by the amount of cramming a candidate had to endure, Bill had pleaded with his dad and mom to take him to a British or an American school.

"But those schools are so expensive," Randy had warned.

"But the Kenyan system is crazy," the boy shot back.

Whatever the misgivings Dad privately harbored, two months after landing at the Jomo Kenyatta International Airport, Bill got into a top British school and immediately set himself apart as the smartest in class. He beat the kids in just about every subject…except IT.

"Still love your school, Bill?"

"I do, Dad. But when I'm done there I wanna go to a school in the U.K., maybe Liverpool, and become a lawyer."

"Do wanna be a doctor?"

"Yuck!"

In spite of the pain in his heart, Randy laughed and slapped Bill affectionately on the back. "What's so yucky about being a doc, son?"

"Blood."

"Just that?"

"Poop!"

"Well—?"

"I'm just not cut out to be a doctor, Dad. I wanna be a lawyer."

"Why Law?"

"Money, Paps!"

"That's not a good reason."

"Fame?"

Randy laughed again. He was impressed by the profession Bill had his eye on. In Kenya there were only three professions that seemed to matter—Law, Medicine and

Engineering. And what was stunning was that in spite the university-level training most students acquired, most of them left such glorified institutions without the ability to initiate or found any business. They sought jobs in already established organizations. Business thought-leaders feared that if such a trend persisted, a time would come when Kenya's jobless rates would hit the roof and keep rising. That's when Luciferain agents would be an even more ominous force in the hands of blood-thirsty occultists, leave alone now!

"Look, Bill," Randy finally said. The two were nearing the gate and Randy suddenly became pensive again. "Don't go into anything because you want money from it; go into it because in it you see a way to earn a living as you fulfill the role God put you in this world for."

"God? You think He put me here for a reason?"

Randy nodded. "He put all of us here for a reason."

"What's yours, Dad?"

Randy reached the gate and was about to open it, but decided Bill's question was too important to ignore. Taking the boy's hand, he said, "Son, I have a story to tell you, but not now. Remind me tomorrow, when you come back from school, to walk you through the story of my life. You will be amazed."

"It will tell me about your purpose in life?"

Randy nodded somberly. He knew that the time to confront his demons of the past had finally come. What he failed to sense was that by coming to Nairobi he had brought his young family into a city under the tight grip of devious, determined Satanists.

Randy was about to come face to face with the flamboyant disciples of the prince of darkness—that ancient dragon!

Four

Vivian collapsed onto her spongy bed. She couldn't believe the swiftness with which her world had fallen apart. This wasn't supposed to happen. Spreading her arms and looking at the ceiling, she wondered why things never seemed to go her way. How could such a beautiful romance be ruined by Kate's colossal carelessness just when it was beginning to feel so sweet? Couldn't she have said something to throw Randy off?

The cell phone rang.

Vivian, perplexed by the turn of events, jumped off the bed and dashed to the living room, where she'd inadvertently forgotten the phone. Finally picking on a fifth ring, she said, "Why are you calling me back?"

But it wasn't Kate; it was her husband, Jerome. Jerome was a tall, slender guy who enjoyed the fast life. Born into a family of a technocrat, he had lived a life most kids in Kenya could only dream of. At only nine, his busy parents had shipped him off to a boarding school and kept him there through primary education. He then went to a provincial secondary school, from where he emerged with strong grades but decided not to go to any of the mushrooming universities in Kenya, instead electing to go into professional training.

"Why are you dodging university education?" his miffed father had asked.

"Because I wanna make money!"

"Money?"

"Watch me, Dad. I'm gonna be rich!"

Dad had watched and Jerome's gamble had paid off handsomely. Within a year of completing his professional training as an accountant, he had worked briefly at the same time as he had started a string of businesses in Nairobi. His largest business, by far, was a lucrative car imports one; it brought in quick, big money. Then there were other less lucrative but just as money-minting. Because of the sudden and dramatic success of the youthful guy, he had decided it was time to get married.

"Marry? Why now?" his confounded dad had bristled when Jerome first slapped the subject on the table.

"This is my decision alone to make, Dad," he had thundered back. "I will take full responsibility for whatever might go wrong." Within months of that solemn declaration, plans had hit top gear. Jerome was getting married to a girl from Kendu-Bay; a girl who was pretty, but very young. To most dismayed villagers, this was unthinkable. Was this what the restless youth of today schemed in their idle hours? Couldn't they wait to grow up before getting married?

"It is a horrible idea, my son," Jerome's cautious mother had weighed in, adding her voice to that of her fuming husband and other less-than-impressed relatives.

Jerome had responded with his own question. "What do you want me to wait for?"

"Do you even know the girl well?" Mama had asked.

"I've even visited her home," he had fired back.

"So this is a done deal, huh?"

It was. Once Jerome's mind was made up, he was not one to change it. Like his father and uncles—and other male members of his wider clan—he was tough and coldly unbendable. He loved a world in which his word was final and stubborn facts never intruded to knock down his thinking. And whenever he was wrong, he preferred not to be told so; he would figure it out himself and turn a corner without the verbal help of lesser mortals.

Tonight Jerome was calling because he was held up in town. A meeting that should have ended by 7:00 p.m. had acquired momentum and was rolling on; so to play nice he was calling home to let Vivian know he would be running late. That's what a nice husband would do, right? What Jerome found on the line, though, was a pissed off Vivian. She said, "Kate, I asked why you are calling back?"

"Sweetheart, it's Jerome, not Kate," her hubby said. "Is there a problem between you and Kate again?"

"Nope," Vivian said curtly. "Just the usual crap."

"The usual crap, huh?" Though Jerome wasn't persuaded, he said it was okay and hung up, but he made a mental note to ask about the matter later. He knew that Kate and Viv didn't just fight for nothing.

Vivian left the living room and hobbled back to the bedroom. Fearful that her evening was sliding steadily into a pile of mess, she decided to get out of the house and drive up to Hurlingham, where she would take a cup of warm chocolate at the Java in Yaya Centre, then come back home right around nine o'clock, in time to meet her husband.

It was about 7:30 p.m. when Vivian set out in the family car. The silver Prado was a state-of-the-art Japanese truck. It boasted power tinted windows, power seats, a showy sunroof and wheels of chrome. The steering was set in a manner that allowed it three positions, depending on the whims of the driver. And the black seats were leather, completing a picture of a car that Vivian's neighbors always warned thieves would go after one day. That that day had never come was something Vivian was thankful for and told friends she didn't take for granted.

Starting off at the parking lot at Kiwi, the apartment community just off of Milimani Road, Vivian turned left and rolled down past Galaxy Hotel, Cornerstone Bank, the Remnant Church headquarters to the left, and on down to Integrity Centre, which stood to her right and had shed off some of the luster that made it a thing of wonder when it housed Trade Bank. As she cruised past that building, shaped like a drowning ship, she sneered and whispered—*What integrity?*

Of course Kenya was consistently rated one of the most corrupt countries in the world. With leaders who had perfected the art of cold impunity and a populace that was too docile to demand a roll of heads whenever scandalous robbery of public coffers took place, the nation had reached the point where everybody's conscience was dead. Nobody cared about the integrity of Kenya.

But that was during the days of men who were appointed to protect swindlers who had turned the East African nation into a swamp of corruption. The days of PLO were ahead, when the country would take the fight to the thieves and drive most out of business. Until then, though, integrity was just a word that reminded Kenyans of the nation's inability to confront the monster that had spread its tenacious tentacles as far deep as the Free Primary Education coffers!

Vivian sped down Milimani Road and took a sharp right into Valley Road. As she blended in with the traffic speeding uphill, she thought of her own integrity. Was there any left? The soft gospel tune that played in the background only served to make the moment more poignant. She needed answers. The question was—*was it true, what geneticists had claimed, that some people were born with a genetic predisposition to be same-sex attracted?* If it was, didn't God have a case to answer? *How*

*could He—an all-knowing God—have created men and women
and deliberately allowed a mix of genetics to set some on a path
to be attracted to members of their same sex? Why in the world
would a conscientious God do that?*

Noting that there were lots of cars speeding up Valley
Road and none at all from the Shell at the Pan Afric Hotel,
Vivian hit Valley Road and sped up the hill that gave the area its
name—Upper Hill. Within seconds of pressing full throttle the
accelerator, she left Valley Road Baptist behind and was fast
approaching the roundabout that intersected that busy road and
Argwings Kodhek. Amazed by how confusing things could
suddenly be, she slowed down as she approached the
roundabout, then pressed the accelerator again to head toward
Yaya. She was coming out here because she desperately needed
a quiet time to reflect on life—her life. She wanted to think.

A few minutes after leaving behind the Valley Road-
Argwings Kodhek roundabout, Vivian came to the main gate at
Yaya Centre and grabbed a parking ticket. And though there
were dozens of cars parked there tonight, she managed to get a
spot. She parked and dashed into the magnificent building.

Built back in the eighties by a politician from the Rift
Valley who was a top powerbroker in the then administration,
the building was one of the most prestigious in Nairobi. Apart
from the fact that it stood on prime land, in an upscale
neighborhood, it was also frequented by the crème de la crème of
Kenya. It was the kind of place one ran into folks whose faces
graced the dailies and others made the cover of some of
Nairobi's glitziest magazines.

The shops and restaurants that did business within the
centre had a steady flow of clients and seemed to do very well,
judging by the stock of goods on shelves and the volume of

customers in there to check them out. It wasn't a normal thing to see a business want to relocate or sink within the centre. Yaya was a security unto itself for businesses.

Java was straight ahead.

Vivian walked briskly to the American-owned restaurant whose proprietor had just been jailed after he was found to have molested Kenyan women workers of the fast-growing chain. The burly American was sentenced to twenty years behind bars. The length of that sentence seemed unthinkable for a national of the United States, but the presiding judge, an icy woman who smiled only through gritted teeth, was out to make a statement. That statement was this—crime is crime!

Once in the fashionable restaurant, Vivian took a seat by the side table, where she was sure to sit alone. Tonight she didn't want company at all; it was her time to soul-search.

A slender waitress walked up to her with a broad smile and tried to give her the menu.

"No, thanks," she said. "Just a cup of chocolate."

"It'll be just a minute."

"Thanks," Vivian said.

As she waited, she thought about the Remnants she'd seen their church along Milimani Road. What did those people believe? She had two sisters who were married to Remnants, but they were unable to coherently articulate what their church taught or even why they believed it. And not only that, Vivian had lived with one of them when she first came to Nairobi and had never liked what she saw in her older sister. The woman was moody 24/7, snobbish and proud. Married to a high-flying architect in the city, she never wanted to mingle with the lowly and talked only to people who drove sleek cars and lived a certain way. What Vivian couldn't understand was how people who went to church and claimed to be Remnants could be so unchristian.

Then there was her other sister. This one was sweet and kind like a baby panda, but went to church only because her husband was an elder there, whatever that meant. Whenever Vivian asked her why she was a member of a church she didn't really care for, she said she did it for her husband and children.

"Children? They like the church?" Vivian would ask.

"I don't care whether they like it or not, Viv," the sister would quip. "All I know is that the Remnants have the best programs for children and they pay keen attention to the growth and development of a child, that's all."

"And what's up with the *elder* thing?" Vivian would ask.

"Oh that? That is a group of men who are elected annually to serve the local Remnant churches as decision-makers."

"Yeah, but what do they have to decide?"

Vivian's sister would at that point shrug nervously, then say, "Why don't you ask your brother-in-law?"

But Vivian had never bothered to ask. Maybe she should have. Had she, she would have learnt that elders were a critical factor in the Remnant Church structure. These men—and in some cases women—literally helped the pastors run the church. And in cases where a pastor ran multiple churches, the Head Elder ran the church.

"Ma'am, your chocolate is ready," the waitress said.

Vivian turned and looked at her and wondered how pretty she was. Dressed in the usual maroon top and black pair of trousers that Java staff wore, she had on a set that defined the curves in her slender frame to a T. She was light and had a cute gap between her upper teeth. With her ready smile and the figure-emphasizing belt she had on, Vivian thought she was a breathtaking beauty.

"Enjoy," the waitress said and walked away.

Still shooting lustful glances her way, Vivian muzzled a feeble thank you, which the waitress never really heard, then reached out for the steaming drink.

Now alone, Vivian went back to the Remnants. What was it about them? What made them tick? And how come she couldn't stand them? Was it because of her husband, who was a practicing believer but did funny things?

Or was it because of her boss, who was a lesbian like her?

Over at the office, Jerome was attending a meeting with a woman who called him frequently, right around meal time. More than once, Vivian had protested the calls, but Jerome had waved them off, calling them nothing but business.

One night, however, Vivian had walked into the apartment at an hour Jerome hadn't expected her home and overheard their conversation. It was as steamy as it was open. She heard them plan a candle-lit dinner at Babylon. Later that evening she had clandestinely followed them to the Babylon, in Lavington, where she heard them discuss something strange; something about fabulous wealth and power; something about praise and worship for Lucifer—the angel of light!

Stunned and hurt, she had slipped away without them noticing her and decided never to ask Jerome about the incident.

There was no need. There was a better way to deal with a sleazy, conniving husband. She was going to revenge.

Vengeance is mine!

FIVE

The text was short.

Viv, Randy and Bill are back!

Vivian looked at the phone, trying to read Kate's mind through the prism of the sms, but she couldn't. Why was Kate telling her about Randy and Bill? Her chocolate drink was delicious, but it just wasn't the same tonight. Something about it was off. She recalled the two times she'd been to this Java and the drink had been nothing short of mesmerizing. It had been kind to the lips, friendly to the stomach and magic to a weary soul. So what was off tonight?

Vivian picked up the cell phone and pressed again.

Viv, Randy and Bill are back!

This time Vivian didn't dismiss the text with a contemptuous wave of the hand. Kate was passing a message. Putting the phone into her bag and lifting her eyes to the TV screen—where Oprah wannabe Tyra Banks was admonishing teenage American kids about their disrespectful ways—she tried hard to think of any reason why Kate would find it necessary to warn her about the return of the two boys in her life. Of course it was important to warn about Randy; that way Vivian would know not to call the rest of the evening. But what about Bill? Why warn her about the boy?

That's when it hit her. She remembered the evening she had dropped Kate off and they had kissed in the car, oblivious to the boy watching them through the window from his second-floor room. The kiss had been passionate and long; and Bill had seen it all. It was when they were done and were crawling back to their senses that Kate had stepped out of the car and caught the curtains drawing shut. Frightened that the boy had seen them, she had slammed back into her seat and told Vivian what had just happened.

"You're lying," Vivian had said horrified and scandalized.

"That curtain just shut, gal!"

"Look, just go in there and pretend all is well. Should the boy bring it up, tell him it's our way of saying goodbye."

Kate had thought about that advice for a second, then she had said, "What if he tells his dad?"

"We'll deal with it when it happens," Vivian had counseled.

Recalling that evening, Vivian pulled out her cell phone again and this time, with a trembling hand, read the message slowly.

Viv, Randy and Bill are back!

Okay I get it, Vivian thought. Bill was out with Randy. That's it. Stunned by the way things were continuing to spiral out of hand, Vivian picked up the decorated ceramic cup and was intent on gulping down the rest of its contents, then run home to beat Jerome there. But just as she was about to kiss the cup to her lips, a dark Mercedes Benz pulled in. A lover of flashy cars, Vivian set the cup back on the table to admire the chrome-wheeled machine and to see who would come out of it. She wanted to see how the person was dressed, how he or she walked and what end of Yaya he or she would go to.

The Mercedes Benz crawled slowly to a dignified halt just two slots away from Vivian's truck. In between the truck and the Benz was another truck; this one shiny silver. It was an American brand that was imposing but not so popular in Nairobi. Because of where it was parked, it neatly separated Vivian's truck from the Benz that had just parked. And because its windows were tinted, Vivian couldn't see the person inside. Even the bright security lights at the lot didn't help.

As Vivian waited, she steered her eyes back to the screen, where one of the girls Tyra Banks was scolding was now on her feet screaming her lungs out. She was saying—*my mother is a fool! I don't know my father and I don't want to know him! You are a wimp, Mom! How dare you bring me here when you are no better than me?*

"Oh my God," Vivian whispered. "What's wrong with American kids? How can they be so nasty?"

But was it the unruly American kids she should have worried about or Nairobi couples? As her eyes slowly veered away from the screen and back to the Benz, she watched the door slowly open. By her count, it had taken whoever was about to step out about five minutes to accomplish that task. Because of the bright lights, Vivian saw the shoes gleaming on the passenger side first. They were a man's. Within seconds, the man stepped out fully, shut the effortless door, then whisked to the driver's side to open the door. When he did, a lady stepped out and the man gave her his hand.

From her vantage point, Vivian saw it all and wondered why Jerome never had such courtesy. Had love grown so cold between them that they couldn't be romantic toward each other anymore? Or was it because of that woman she had seen with her husband in Babylon?

The couple walked slowly toward the main entrance, engrossed in the sweet company of each other, feeling as though life was a staircase that led from one lofty height to another of romantic bliss. What Vivian couldn't understand, as she stole quick glances at the couple, was why some men and women were lucky enough to find true love and lasting happiness in marriage when Jerome and her were perpetually struggling. How could it be that after only five years of marriage her husband was willing to see other women? And how was it that once she had confirmed that Jerome was nursing an affair she had never forgiven him but had gone out on a free-for-all steamy revenge mission? Who between them had ruined the romance at home?

The elegant woman, with her arm in the tall man's arm, was light and about as tall as the man. They were now under a shade and Vivian could only make out the fact that they were in each other's arms and were kissing. Amused, she wondered why they just couldn't wait to get home to bury the urge. But when she saw a girl in a blue school uniform walk toward the kissing couple, Vivian turned away and looked at the screen again. The Tyra Banks show was now over and the credits were crawling on the screen, a soothing Mozart in the background. Vivian didn't want to be a witness to how the girl reacted upon seeing two adults kiss under a shade at a parking lot. Wasn't this absurd?

She thought about Bill again. Kate's little boy. Was there any difference between what this girl was about to see and what Bill had seen the evening Kate and her had passionately kissed? And though the boy had never told his dad, should that have been reason enough for the relationship between her and Kate to swing on unperturbed?

Finally the couple started walking again. Being close to the entrance, it didn't take long before they got into Yaya and disappeared in the crowd. Wherever they were going, a lot of folks would be looking at them in awe, Vivian thought. They were a picture perfect portrait of what love was about. They were rich. Happy. And knew how to enjoy life. *Man, would Jerome and I ever get to this point?*

But now that the Mercedes Benz couple was gone and the Tyra Banks Show was over, Vivian called the waitress to give her the bill. Promptly brought, she paid it and was about to get off her seat and head out when the couple walked right into the Java and walked toward her, obviously whispering sweet nothings to each other. They walked on until they came to a point where a mesmerized Vivian couldn't avoid looking at them directly. It was at that point that she realized why the two had looked so familiar.

It was Jerome and the Babylon woman!

———

When Randy and Bill got home, Kate was in the bedroom—and though she appeared not to have known they were back, Randy wasn't fooled. He knew she'd been watching through the window and was probably in touch with Vivian through the time they were gone. But tonight Randy didn't want *matata*, so he was going to have dinner then go to bed and would behave as if everything was okay the rest of the evening.

The moment he and Bill came through the living room door, they whispered something, then Bill went to his room. But Randy, aware Bill would be listening in on the mama-papa conversation, lingered in the hallway, then opened the bedroom door only when he had ascertained that the boy hadn't tiptoed behind him. Once in the bedroom, he said, "It's a refreshing walk Bill and I just had. What's for dinner?"

Kate looked perplexed. Was this a way for a pissed-off husband to behave? She had expected him to come back growling like a wounded lion and threaten her with instant divorce. Why was he reading from a different script?

"No dinner for us?"Randy pressed.

"I've made something."

"Chicken?"

Kate's tears formed. She didn't like this. When was Randy going to explode so they could deal with this matter? Since childhood, Kate had been the kind of girl who never appreciated such games. Rather than subject her to silent treatment, she'd have much rather been caned or beaten so that the matter ended promptly. Mind games were childish and, in her opinion, accomplished nothing. Didn't Randy know she detested this approach to problem-solving?

Randy walked toward her and took her hand. Edging in to plant a kiss, he said, "Made fish?"

Kate shook her head.

"Then what did you make?"

Kate pulled away from him gently, then sat on the bed. Boldly, she invited him to drop in next to her. As soon as he did, she whispered, "Sweetheart, there is no need pretending things are okay between us; they are not. I know Bill has told you about the evening he saw Viv and I kiss in the driveway. I don't know how to take any of the mistakes I've made back other than to say I'm so sorry."

Randy reached out and put an arm around her. "Kate, I was mad and confused when I first heard about this, but I'm not mad anymore. And Bill has not told me anything." He looked her in the eye. "That boy is so protective of you; did you really think he would tell me anything unpleasant about you?"

Kate was moved. "He didn't?"

"Look, even now, as we separated in the hallway, he just told me to treat his mommy well!"

Kate wiped a tear.

"Which makes me wonder, Kate. Why have you done this to us? Is there anything lacking in our relationship that would make you seek love in the arms of another woman?" Randy's voice was unusually low-key and groggy as he spoke. "Have I let you down in any way?"

Kate shook her head. "It's all my fault, Randy."

"So where do we go from here?"

Kate knew that the journey back to normal in her family would not be an easy one. She had blown the trust of her son, who had seen her kiss a person other than his father, and blown the trust of her husband, who had just discovered that the wife he had loved and been dedicated to all along was a lesbian. Aware such wounds didn't heal overnight, she said, "If you can find it in your heart to forgive me, I will walk away from my lesbian lifestyle and make you proud."

"How about Vivian?" Randy asked.

Kate took her time. She didn't know why Randy was asking about Vivian. Was he afraid Vivian would cast a spell so powerful that Kate would never walk away from it? Or was there a part of him that was beginning to find the woman who had lured his wife into lesbianism curious? Fearing that Randy would seek revenge for her betrayal, Kate looked him in the eye and said, "Randy, please forgive me?"

Randy took her in his arms and promised they would work on this matter together—as a husband and wife. But even as he made the sweeping promise, his mind was on Vivian. Vivian the beauty queen.

Where was she now?

Six

Vivian was crying.

And back in her bedroom, Kate couldn't believe what was going on either. Only hours ago, Vivian had disrespectfully shoved her out, literally telling her she had no apologies to make for trying to break Kate's family. She was as disrespectful and as remorseless as could be. Not more than three hours later, she was now calling with tears in her eyes, her voice breaking. What was Kate to make of this? Turning to Randy for approval, Kate finally exhaled in a staggered fashion, then said, "Viv, what's the matter with you today?"

"I caught them again!"

"Caught who?" Kate asked.

"Jerome and the Babylon woman!"

Kate didn't talk. Wasn't this too much for one day? Just when she thought things might finally be quieting down, here was another bombshell. Why was life like this? Why was it that when trouble started it had a way of snowballing, creating a convoluted mess that took months to set straight?

"Gal, did you hear what I just said?" Vivian pressed, her sobs more pronounced now.

Not willing to be kept out of the loop this time round, Randy whispered in Kate's ear. He asked her to turn on the speakerphone.

"Kate?"

"I'm here, gal. It's just ... it's just that what you said completely blew me away. Those two still had a thing for each other?"

"They came in a sharp Mercedes Benz," Vivian said.

"Came? Came where?"

"To the Java in Yaya."

Kate frowned. "What in the world were you doing there?"

Vivian recounted the way her evening had played out, describing in detail how lonely she had felt and how her mind had taken flight to things she had never thought of before.

"Like what?" Kate asked.

"Suicide."

"What!" Kate became fearful. Whether she liked it or not, Vivian was the best friend she had in Nairobi and she didn't wanna lose her. A recluse whose life was marked by one disappointing friendship after another, Kate had never managed to maintain friendships beyond the first quarrel. Whenever anybody crossed words with her over any issue, it was the end. *Kaboom!* Finally aware of this trait, Kate had decided not to have friends; instead she would make her husband her best friend. Things played out in that fashion until she met Vivian; and because Vivian was willing to put up with her erratic ways, the new friendship grew into something tight, then into an affair.

What Kate never knew was that while she was drawn to Vivian because Viv was pretty and caring, Vivian was drawn to her because Viv wanted to avenge Jerome's deceitful ways—that reckless husband who just a week ago she had caught in Babylon with the woman who called him every evening at meal time. As the Kate-Viv affair had blossomed, though, both women had forgotten about the moral dangers lesbianism posed and saw in it a legitimate avenue for dealing with life's bitterest edges. Its satanic darkness wore off. It was better than going into rehab, they thought—and actually, more fun.

"Suicide? Don't even go there, Viv. You and I are too old to talk about crap like suicide. You can't kill yourself over Jerome's affair; can't you look in the mirror?"

"What mirror?"

"The mirror, Viv. *Kio*. What do you see?"

"Oh, shut up!"

"Exactly," Kate said and managed a forced laugh. "You and I are not innocent either. We have done to Randy and Jerome exactly what Jerome has done to you."

"Oh, so this is payback?"

"Is it?" Kate was momentarily amused by the irony. First, it was Vivian who had paid back when she caught Jerome with the Babylon woman; now it was Jerome paying back, huh?

Vivian said, "Why would Jerome payback, it's not like he knows anything about us?"

"True, but he knows you've not been the same woman since you busted him. He must think you've been seeing someone, Viv. Have you thought of that?"

Kate looked at Randy with eyes that said *please-let-me-turn-off the-speakerphone* and Randy nodded and walked out of the bedroom to give them badly needed privacy. Following him to be sure he was finally gone, Kate whispered, "Viv, what's wrong with you? What in the world are you doing at Yaya this late?"

"Drinking chocolate."

"Chocolate indeed! So now that you know your man is still seeing the Babylon cutie, what are you going to do?"

"Crucify him!"

"Gal, get serious. I don't have much time; my boys are waiting in the dining room."

Vivian said, "Sweetheart, I was devastated when I saw Jerome with that woman. It broke my heart. I thought the affair had long ended. Anyway, now that it's still on, I'll just have to do what I've got to do."

"Which is?"

Vivian walked out of Yaya and was stunned to see how dark it was outside. Opening the door and jumping into the truck, she said, "I'll just have to find a man to love me this time."

"A man? I thought you hate men?"

Vivian let a cynical laughter come through her throat, touch her lips, then she said, "I told you I hated men because I wanted you, Kate. I wanted you to be my partner and figured you would never agree if you thought I was a double."

"A double? What in the world is a dou..."

"A double is a woman who loves men and women," Vivian said, cutting her off.

"So you love men after all?"

Vivian started the truck and maneuvered it away from the parking lot. She took a third look at the dark Mercedes Benz before she pulled out. In that instant, she realized she had seen that car parked where Jerome worked, but had never bothered to find out who owned it. She'd assumed one of the bosses there did.

"Viv?"

"Of course I love men!"

Kate felt stabbed in the back. She recalled the many times at the office she had asked Vivian about the string of men who came there to see her and Vivian had always said they were delusional men who couldn't read her hatred for them on her face. So it was a lie?

"Look here, Kate. I did what I did because I wanted to punish Jerome. I thought he would feel humiliated if he found out I was dating a woman," Vivian said.

"So that time you told me you wanted to marry me...what was that about?"

The truck was now rolling down Argwings Kodhek. Soon Vivian was gonna be at the roundabout. Slowing down to avoid turning at a high speed, she said, "That was just something I said. Gal, why do we have to go over this stuff now anyway?"

"Because you are dishonest," Kate blurted.

"Huh?"

"I don't ever wanna see you again!"

Vivian laughed. "Does that mean I'm fired?"

Kate suddenly faced a dilemma. She couldn't just fire Vivian. That loudmouth was capable of causing so much trouble.

"Are you firing me?"

"I'm not!"

"I didn't think you could just fire me," Vivian said. "And by the way, gal, while you've been romancing me, who has been romancing Randy ... or you think he was too blind to catch on to your distractions? Ever bothered to find out who kept him busy?"

That was the final blow. Kate hung up and threw the phone on the bed. She walked slowly to the dining room and sat next to Randy, but she never served even though she found the guys eating the food she had just prepared and had looked forward to eating with them. Then, just moments after getting to the dining room, Kate excused herself and went to the bedroom.

"What's the matter now, Daddy?" Bill asked, looking at his dad quizzically. "Is Mama okay?"

"To be honest with you, I left her talking to Vivian over the phone; that's all I know. What surprises me, though, is that you knew about your mom and Vivian but never told me anything. How long did you intend to keep this from me?"

Bill dropped his fork on the table and shut his eyes. "How did you find out?" he asked.

"Your mom told me."

Thinking swiftly, Bill said, "Dad, don't you think it was better for Mama to tell you this herself than for me to do it?"

The boy had a point. Nodding in agreement, Randy took a final bite of the chicken, then got up and followed Kate to the bedroom. As soon as the door opened, he said, "What does she want?"

Kate turned. "It's not about her I'm worried, it's about Jerome."

"Huh? Why?"

"No, Randy, I've not slept with Jerome; and no, he's not my boyfriend. The thing is—he's been dating women neither Vivian nor I know. I'm just worried that—"

"—that you may have caught AIDS?"

Kate looked down. Was it worth it? Was a little fun with Vivian worth subjecting her family through this? Pulling the comforter over her head, she wished Randy a good night and cried softly. What she couldn't understand was how a pastor's daughter had allowed herself to get into such a mess. Could anybody blame this too on the devil?

———

Vivian got home and went straight to the bedroom. This evening had turned into nothing but wasteland. She just wanted to collapse onto the bed and forget Kate, forget Randy, forget Bill and Jerome, and definitely forget that sleazy Babylon woman. But just before she could draw the comforter over her head, Jerome stormed into the bedroom and said, "Viv, we've got to talk!"

Vivian turned instantly. "Goodness, you scared me!"

"Whatever you saw, it wasn't what you think it is."

"I didn't see anything," Vivian said.

Jerome dropped onto the bed and drew a deep breath. The bedroom was spacious, with generous blinds on opposite walls. It was painted a soft, soothing cream, which made the walls recede and gave the impression of an open, wider space than its length and width actually vouched for. It was carpeted wall-to-wall and boasted some of the softest fluorescent tubes to grace a bedroom in this city. It was a perfect mirror of the high taste the couple brought to life and to everything they did.

Vivian said, "Who is that woman?"

Jerome had all along known that one day he would have to tell Vivian about Carol and had prepared his answer carefully, but tonight, after what Vivian had seen, that answer seemed contrived and wholly inappropriate. He had to think of a better lie to avoid bringing up his tight links with the powerful Luciferians.

Still, he sensed that tonight marked a turning point.

SEVEN

"Viv, I met that woman in Mombasa."

Jerome knew he was in a fix. Only moments ago, Vivian had categorically told him that she knew everything and that this was his only chance to come clean. Truth was, though, Vivian didn't know a thing but was using this time-tested ruse to dig gold out of a guy who tonight showed incredible vulnerability after his wife had said she had seen him kiss the Babylon woman and lead her into Yaya.

"Her name is Carol," Jerome added without a prompt.

"Just Carol?"

Jerome bit his lip. This was gonna be a long night, he could tell. "Sweetheart, I don't know her other name."

"Don't worry, I do," Vivian deadpanned.

Pissed, Jerome said, "Why are you asking me about her if you've done your homework and know everything already?"

"To determine whether I can continue to trust you or not."

"Fine. Her name is Carol. I met her in Mombasa more than three years ago. My boss had sent me to Mombasa and we met in a restaurant owned by the same hotel I had spent the night in. As I recall now, she was as flabbergasted as I was about the slow pace of everything in the coastal city. It felt like everybody was on vacation there.

"Anyway, we started talking about Mombasa, Nairobi, Kisumu, Nakuru, Eldoret and I was stunned by her comprehensive knowledge of life in those cities and towns. She was an encyclopedia of everything Kenyan; from food to clothing to tribes to nightlife... After about an hour and no food on the table, we walked out of the restaurant and back to the hotel. As we were walking through the lobby, Carol told me she had some little food we could share in her room. Seeing no harm in the offer, I obliged.

"I got into Carol's room and sure enough there was some food. We ate the cakes and oranges and drank some water. Then I asked her to let me go. It was at that time that Carol got up, walked to me and sat on my lap and told me that if I became her friend, she would make me a wealthy young man."

"Did you let her sit?"

"I did."

"And—?"

"Viv, the woman, over the next three days, took me to places I never knew existed in this world. She took me to buildings where I met naked people—men and women—worshiping some tall, dark figure at the sky-blue corner. I saw people who she said were prominent folks in Mombasa, Nairobi and the rest of Kenya. They all bowed in reverence to the figure. When she saw that I was scared stiff, she stood right next to me and whispered something strange."

Vivian slapped away the comforter. "What did she say?"

"That all dominion and glory was to that figure; nobody got rich in this world except through him."

"Huh? *Him*?"

"She told me that God created this vast world, but lost it to the beautiful angel, Lucifer. Lucifer, according to Carol, wrestled the world from God and is out to show humanity how unjust God is by presenting a coherent case against Him in the court of universal opinion. It is the great controversy; a controversy of the ages; a controversy Lucifer will win!"

"My God!"

"And then Carol invited me to a second meeting. It was at that meeting that she told me initiates into the movement were baptized. The baptism consisted of a string of rituals that culminated in the drinking of human blood and a commission to the new members."

"Jerome!"

"It's all true, Vivian. You wanted the truth; I'm giving you the truth as it was passed on to me by Carol."

"Where does the blood come from?" Viv asked.

"Okay, this will shock you. Have you heard of folks who claim they are serial killers? That they are occultists? That is the blood used. Those guys are under the command of a secret power structure that meets in various cities and towns in Kenya, Uganda and Tanzania. But there are other similar structures throughout Africa and the world. Those serial killers and occultists are under strict instructions to deliver blood each month to a cell leader. What that means is—they must kill one person per month. That is why you always hear them talk about an urge to kill.

"But that is just the beginning. The bigger deal rests with those in leadership in business and politics. Those guys, because of the power they wield, are required to collect even more blood. That is why you see a nation like ours in repeated cycles of violence that though our leaders could control, they somehow chose to let play out."

"Are you serious?" Vivian asked.

"Wagalla, the land clashes, the political murders over the years, the 2007 disputed elections… the list runs deep; do you think those were ordinary disputes? And do you know how much blood was collected? Vivian, my dear, what Carol told me was that this world belongs to Lucifer and is run according to the dictates of Lucifer."

"Satan, you mean?"

Jerome thought for a second, then he nodded. "Most Christians call him Satan, but his followers don't call him that; to them he is the ruler of the universe. And by the way, most Christians in this country do not know just what they are up against. The principalities of darkness are organized and deadly; their approach is subtle but assured. They have agents in the offices, at the playgrounds, in the media, in the government and even in the church. It's because of their pervasive influence that I asked Carol what she thought of Christians."

"What did she say?" Vivian asked guarded.

"She said that the Luciferians..."

"The what? Did you say Luciferians?"

Jerome nodded, finally feeling a bit at ease. Truth was better than lies, he thought. "Luciferians is what they call themselves. It's an effort to restore the good name of the angel most Christians now call the devil, Satan, the deceiver and other names like that. He is god!"

"So they think Christians are ... crazy?" Vivian pressed.

"They think they have managed to completely confuse and outfox the Christians. They have made Christians focus on all the wrong things, like jewelry, the right day of worship, right foods to eat and divisive doctrines while forgetting what would really make the Church of Christ grow. The Luciferians are on a roll!"

Vivian now sat. No, this didn't feel right. Was it really Jerome she was talking to? Jerome—ever since she started dating him, and right through their marriage—had never been such a smart dude; the guy was dull at best, bored most of the time. Where did he get this occultist stuff from? *My God, or is he one of the Luciferians?*

Vivian said, "Two questions. One, what is it that would make the Church of Christ grow? And two, and I want an honest answer to this. Are you a Luciferian, Jerome?"

Jerome cleared his throat. "Sweetheart, to your first question the answer is—*love*. Wasn't that what Christ said? He said that the greatest commandment was *Love the Lord your God with all your heart and your neighbour as you love yourself*. But just look around you...do you see love in the church? The Luciferians have infiltrated the church; they have caused brother to slight brother, sister to hate sister and pastors to scheme against one another. The Church of Christ has become a cross upon which those who come to seek solace and love are crucified and their bodies left hanging on a modern-day Golgotha!

"To your second question the answer is even simpler— No, I'm not a Luciferian. Look, if you are wondering how I came to know the things I know, you have to remember that I've been to Mombasa many times. I've seen things I can't tell you about in one night. If you wanna know more, you gonna have to have a date with me."

Vivian, in spite of the fear that had steadily built in her as Jerome recounted the Luciferian game-plan, smiled, then she shot her final question. "Have you slept with her?" *Is she a Slut for Satan?*

———

Randy knew that Kate was pretty exhausted. He waited until she had cried herself to sleep, then picked up the phone and dialed.

At the other end, Vivian, just coming off a scary story session with Jerome, answered on a second ring. She had no clue who was calling because she had never received a call from Randy.

Randy said, "Viv, this is Randy."

Vivian froze. *Jeez.* This just wasn't a good time to talk. "Can it wait till tomorrow?" she asked.

"It can't," Randy said in a suggestive whisper and Vivian had to sheepishly turn to look at Jerome.

"Well, what is it that can't wait?" she asked.

"Something very urgent!"

"That's okay, but we'll just have to arrange something in the morning. Goodnight!" She cut the line.

"Who was that?" Jerome asked.

"A guy at the office. He wants some work typed up for an 8:30 meeting, which again I'm supposed to arrange."

"Your job stinks!"

"Thanks for the compliment."

Jerome got off the bed and said he was going to shower. It was only 10.30 p.m., but it felt like midnight. While he was gone, Vivian picked up the phone and dialed Randy's number. When he answered, Vivian said, "Don't blame me for what's happened, Randy, both your wife and I are at fault here."

"I didn't call to blame you, Viv, just wanted to have lunch."

Vivian couldn't believe it. Randy wanted to have lunch? Wasn't that Nairobi-speak for *I am available?*

"Can we meet at The Palace?" Randy pressed.

Vivian agreed. "Let's make it one."

The moment Randy hung up with Vivian, he shut his eyes in defeat. He knew that he had just opened the floodgates of hell and would soon be swept into an abyss by the gushing waters of deceptive love and stolen romance. But since Kate had done it first, wasn't fair fair? What better revenge was there than to have an affair with the very woman Kate had cheated with? This was sweet!

For Vivian, though, this was just another conquest if it happened. While it would be sweet to avenge Jerome's betrayal with Carol, she felt urged on by a mysterious force to sleep with every man and woman she came across. It was an urge so strong that at times she wondered why she hadn't discovered the glory of *sex* sooner. In fact, if Carol could use it to lure Jerome and other men, why not her?

It was in that hour that Vivian's eyes opened for the first time. It was like a glorious vision. She was shown that *sex* had a goddess. What she wasn't shown yet was that the goddess of sex was the woman she had seen with her husband in Babylon.

Yes, Carol was a knighted Slut for Satan—the goddess of the sect!

EIGHT

Carol was an only child. She was born into a family of peasants in a tiny village along the border of Kenya and Tanzania. Her mother died when she gave birth to the cute girl. That girl grew up under the protective custody of her vigilant father, who doubled up as a struggling farmer and fisherman. Being an only child, a girl for that matter, the proud father was forever watchful who his little girl hung out with and advised boys who were up to no good never to even think of coming close to his precious gem. Dating Carol was suicidal, he warned without letting the boys know just how dangerous it really was.

Growing up in her lonely rural village, Carol turned out to be a remarkable replica of her late mother. Her dad repeatedly told her endearing stories about a mother she only saw in black and white photos on the *okaka*-decorated mud wall. In his good moments, he would even tell Carol about the rhythmic local songs Mama liked to sing, the mouth-watering Luo delicacies she enjoyed making and the secret friends she had across the sprawling village.

Then one night, when Carol was sixteen and had come home for holidays from a school where she was in form two, her drunken father had stormed into her room with his pants all the way down and pleaded to have a moment with her. Stunned, Carol had bolted out of the house and stood in the yard. Carol had waited until things had quieted down, then she had gone back in.

When she got in, she found her dad crying in the living room, talking between sobs with a woman Carol couldn't see. She listened in awe as her father recounted the tough life he'd had to endure since the woman parted, how he had dedicated his life to taking care of their daughter and how things were getting even worse because the girl was now grown and would soon be gone for good. "I'm about to live the loneliest life on earth," Carol had heard him say.

In that deeply emotional moment, Carol was overcome with grief and had tiptoed to her dad, who didn't know she'd been listening, then said, "It will be all right, Father."

Her crying father had looked up and shaken his head. He'd said, "How can it ever be okay? Can't you see that my life will be a nightmare once you are gone?"

"But I'll always visit," she had said.

That night Carol had allowed her dad into her bed and they had done things a father and a daughter should never have. When it was over, the father had looked her in the eye and said, "My dear daughter, from today on you will become the most powerful representative of the church I belong to in East Africa. You will make disciples of anybody you meet and will ensure that our organization grows from strength to strength."

"What organization are you talking about?" Carol had asked. "I thought you were a Catholic?"

"Sweetheart, I'm a crucifix-wearing Catholic by day, a sword-wielding Luciferian by night. If you'll now allow me, I want to show you something."

Together, Carol and Dad walked through the night to an open field about a kilometer from home. When they got there, the old man told her to look at a sleeping hill yonder.

"But it's dark," Carol protested. "I can't see anything."

"Look again."

Carol looked and this time she saw a flaming fire. In the middle of the fire was a dark figure that looked like a man. The figure grew in clarity until his angelic face took shape. His white robe cut through the night like a sharp ray of a morning sun. As they waved, the angelic figure waved back.

"What is that?" Carol asked, fear in her voice.

"The One!"

"The one? Who is The One?"

"The ruler of the earth!"

"Does he have a name?" she asked.

Calmly, her dad said, "Carol, there is a long story I need to tell you. Let us sit under this tree."

"But this is a field, Dad. There is no tre...."

A leafy acacia suddenly appeared and her dad took her hand and led her to it. It was warm and friendly under it. As they sat, he said, "What you and I had in the house was not sex, my girl; it was passing the mantle to the next generation of Luciferians."

"Of what?"

"Luciferians."

"But, Dad, I am a Catholic!"

"True. So am I. But we Luciferians can be anything we want to be." He kept quiet for a while, then he started again. "For instance, did you know that in another life I own a Mercedes Benz and a palatial home in one of the most exclusive suburbs in Nairobi? And did you know that as we speak my jet is parked at Wilson Airport ready for me to board and fly to any part of Eastern African where my boss needs me urgently?"

Carol's breath caught. "Your boss? Who is your boss?"

"I work for Morning Star Limited."

"Never heard of them."

"I know, but you've heard of Ndai, right?"

Suddenly it all fell in place. Ndai was one of the wealthiest men in Kenya; in fact the *East African* had consistently rated him among the wealthiest folks in Africa. But that's not how Carol had come to know him. Carol knew the tycoon through the trendy magazines he owned and the glamorous women's clothing that bore his initial *N.* Ndai was a household name not only in Kenya, but in Uganda, Tanzania, Ethiopia and through most of the Southern African nations.

"So you work for Ndai?" Carol asked.

"I am the *ai* in Ndai."

"Pardon me, what did you say?"

"Let me explain. Ndai is a joint venture that brings together two dynamic individuals. There is *Nd*, which are the beginning letters for the name of the lady standing behind you."

"Behind me?" Carol turned and—as sure as the open skies of Karungu are blue—there was a lady; a tall lady; a lady she knew from pictures on the wall. With tears, she said, "Mama?"

"And then there is *ai* which is me," her dad said.

"So Ndai as in **Nd**eda and **Ai**ro, huh?"

"Got it," Dad said.

Stunned, Carol looked at the two folks who claimed to be her parents and said, "Are you guys saying you own Morning Star?"

"We do!"

"Does that mean Mama has never really been dead?"

The woman said, "Carol, Luciferians never die; we just go from one state to another."

"So where does that leave the story I've been repeatedly told by Dad that you died when I was born?"

The woman said, "Carol, I had work to do. What most people don't realize is that we have a very short time. You see, Christians read their Bibles and the many books written for them by clergy and top theologians, but they can't grasp the urgency of what they read because we have distracted them. We have come up with discotheques, the Internet, pornography, sleazy mags, dirty movies and other forms of distractions to keep them occupied. We just can't afford to let them read their Bibles and focus on Christ."

"So you are also a Luciferian?" Carol asked.

"Your father and I are high priests. Between him and I, we have led thousands of Christians away from Christ. I have slept with many leading pastors and exposed them. I have led many pastors to swindle church money and exposed them. I have planted seeds of disharmony in churches all across this region and caused many young people in churches to question their place in the church hierarchy." She smiled. "Carol, our time is very short. Like the Bible says, when the trumpet of the Lord shall sound time shall be no more…"

"Don't go into that now, Ndeda, just tell her what our goal is," her Dad said, cutting the woman off.

"Our goal is to make sure that when Christ returns, He will find no one on earth who still worships Him ... and if He has to destroy the Luciferains, because He is such a cruel being, we want Him to destroy just about everybody and everything on the face of this earth!"

"My God!"

"As we speak," the woman said, "I have singlehandedly turned Kenya into a nation where people are lovers of money, glorifiers of raw sex and beholden to the trappings of power; a nation where the youth are buried in rabid occultism, porno and pursue careers that ultimately bring personal aggrandizement rather than praise to God."

"Like law?" Carol asked.

"Yes."

"Medicine?"

"Aha!"

"Architecture?"

"You got it," the woman said.

"Are you saying those are evil careers?" Carol asked.

"Nope."

"Well—?"

"What I'm saying is that we have found out over the years that folks who are in those professions are easier to lure away and actually be used in our agenda than folks in lowlier professions. In many churches their ego is bloated; always seeking to be elders, deacons etc. When they fail to get those positions, we use them to wreck havoc in those churches. They become mediums, our undercover agents. It works like magic."

"Fine," Carol said. "So what do you want me to do? What's my place in this grand scheme?"

The woman said, "Behold I make you one of the most beautiful women in the world. I want you to work primarily in Kenya. In this nation your role will be to recruit worthy men to our cause. We want professionals to join our crusade. And because of that huge responsibility we slap on your shoulders, you'll get a nice home in Muthaiga and a Mercedes Benz. You'll also have an active Luciferian Screen to survey the progress of our relentless activities."

"How about school?" Carol asked.

"Forget school now; there's no time for trappings like degrees and papers. In any case, we already have student-agents everywhere."

That very night, Carol had accompanied her peasant father—and the woman (mother) who had showed up mysteriously in the Karungu night—to Nairobi. By the time the trio got home, a sprawling bungalow in Muthaiga, the peasants had turned into aristocrats. From their super expensive footwear to the trendy thread they had on to the glittering godfather Dad had on and the necklace emblazoned with an image of a fallen, shattered cross Mama had on, the duo had transformed themselves from grinding paupers to the wealthiest couple in Kenya.

It was stunning!

Since that dramatic beginning in the open fields of Karungu, Carol had gone on to recruit thousands of men and women into the most mysterious organization in Kenya. There was only one guy who had proved pretty difficult to lure. She was going to give it a final shot. If Jerome couldn't be won over this time, he was gonna have to pay a huge price because she had revealed too much to him already. Too bad it had to come to this. It was now loyalty or death. The choice was his.

Nine

Tonight Kate couldn't sleep. As much as she tried to close her eyes and will herself to snooze away, something kept gnawing at the edges of her thoughts, keeping her in a perpetual state of alertness. But it wasn't until around 2:00 a.m. that she finally gave up her efforts and gently dug an elbow into Randy's ribs with a lament. "Sweetheart, I can't sleep!"

Randy put his arm around her and said, in a soothing voice, "What's the matter, honey?"

"I'm bothered by what Vivian has done to me. How can a friend try to blackmail a friend?"

Randy cleared his throat. He was aware that when his little family lived in Indianapolis, Indiana, Kate had never had friends and never wanted to have any. She had complained that friends were never sincere; that they always broke your heart and hurt your feelings and they didn't care at all. *Friends are about gossip and silly competition.* Since coming back to Kenya, Kate had not moved an inch in her attitude. She had maintained her uncompromising stance—insisted that her only friends were Randy and Bill.

Then she met the dashing office administrator who took her hand and shoved her into a world of same-sex attraction. At first it had been subtle, then it became less subtle, then its sinfulness wore off and it even became fashionable. Now it was at a point it was coming back to haunt her. Worst of all, all the things Vivian had told her were now keeping her awake. Why did she let herself get far off track like this?

"Randy, talk to me. Is Viv really a friend?"

Randy didn't know what to say. But as Kate had battled her betrayal through that moonless night, Randy had gone through a different kind of battle—the battle to win Vivian over. He wanted the woman. He wanted to sleep with her, make her his permanent girlfriend. After all, coming to Nairobi, Randy had noticed that Nairobi had gone the way of California. Everywhere Randy looked he saw men and women at plush city restaurants and hotels and he could tell, just by the way the couples behaved, that they were celebrating stolen love. It was romance on the fast lane. Crazy thing was … he knew that while one husband was with another man's wife at the Koinange Galaxy, the man's wife was also with another woman's husband at Cold Heart.

But what had stunned Randy even more was the infiltration of permissiveness into the church. Born into Christian family, Randy was brought up with strict morals. His father and mother were paragons of virtue; two folks who stayed in love and true to each other right into old age. Because of that traditional approach to matters of marriage, Randy had always been drawn to Christianity's puritanical stance and told friends about his faith whenever he had a chance.

Tonight, however, all he could think about was revenge. How could Kate have betrayed him? How dare she embarrass him like that? But this self-righteousness, he knew only too well, was an effort to justify his desire for revenge and nothing else. The fury he had built in his pounding heart as he repeatedly asked himself that question had only served to make him rationalize his pursuit of an affair with Vivian on the basis that his fellow church members were into affairs as well.

"Randy?"

"Oh, sorry, sweetheart."

"Did you hear me?" Kate asked.

Randy cleared his voice a second time and this time he talked. He said, "Kate, I don't know Vivian that well and I don't know how you two have related in the past. Do you think it's fair for you to now ask me about a woman I know nothing about?"

Kate got offended, but she was gonna keep her cool; after all she deserved what she was getting. Still, she wasn't gonna let Randy get away with a snippy attitude. He was a man. Men were supposed to have answers. She said, "Randy, what I'm asking is not case-specific, okay? I'm asking you a hypothetical question. If a friend blackmailed you, would you continue to consider that person a friend?"

"Kate, to you this is hypothetical, to me it is a case of my wife asking me about a betrayal that is playing out as we speak. Let me ask you a question too. If a friend you love and care for deeply gets involved romantically with someone else, regardless of gender, would you ever consider such a person a friend *again*?"

"No," Kate said.

Randy kissed Kate on the cheek, then he said, "Sweetheart, isn't that what you did to me when you got involved with Vivian?"

Kate slapped away the comforter and came up on her elbow. "Randy, it's true I betrayed you, and it's true that while I did it I wasn't being a friend at all. I'm so sorry. But this I know for sure—that friends don't betray friends!"

Randy agreed in principle, but his mind was made up. What Kate had done had opened the door for him to explore what lay on the other side of matrimonial fidelity. He wanted to find out what other men felt when they had affairs; to see what it felt like to be loved in a way different from the way Kate loved him. But more than anything else, he wanted to get even with Kate; she deserved to be punished for straying.

"Randy?"

"Yes—?"

"Do you know Jerome well?"

Randy was caught off-guard. He hadn't expected Kate to bring that guy into this conversation. What was her motive?

"Ever met him?" Kate pressed.

"We've met, but I don't think we've ever talked beyond casual greetings. Why do you ask?"

"I've been wondering about his trips to Mombasa. He goes there a lot and Viv has no clue what he goes to do. At first it was about a car imports business, then a restaurant business, now he says he runs a busy courier company. What I don't get is why he doesn't just stay there?"

Randy didn't answer.

"Besides, don't you think it's because of his extended stay from Viv when on those trips that Viv got into her crazy lifestyle?"

Randy finally figured out where this talk was going. Kate was making excuses for Vivian, trying to let her off the hook. "You still like her, don't you?" he pointedly asked.

"Not in the old sense, no," she said.

"Meaning?"

"Meaning I intend to relate to her on a professional basis. As my junior and a girl younger than me, I will treat her with respect, but must now have boundaries. I want to be true to my family; true to my God!"

God? Randy came up on his elbow too and managed to sit with extra effort. Was Kate trying to get off the hook easy too? Why was she talking about professionalism and God and Jerome?

"You know, Randy?"

Randy's eyes shut. *Now what?* "Yes—?"

"Vivian told me something I've always wondered about. She said, one day as we walked along Moi Avenue, that three quarters of women in Nairobi are lesbians; that lesbianism has become the weapon of choice against errant husbands. Do you believe her?"

"Looking at what goes on on *Facebook*, I'm inclined to believe her. I've come to realize that many women in Nairobi and Mombasa are indeed same-sex attracted. I've even seen girls openly kiss and embrace suggestively on city streets. Hollywood has caught up with us, Kate."

Kate said, "I'm glad you brought that up. I was actually thinking you and I could start a focused ministry on *Facebook* and *Twitter*; reach the youth of Nairobi where they congregate."

"Are you saying they are not in churches anymore?"

"It's not a secret, Randy. You've heard the lament of Pastor Ogwoka of the Remnant Church. Whenever he invites the youth to afternoon events very few show up, and during the well advertised youth camp meetings, hardly any come back to listen to preachers imported from the States or the U.K. at colossal amounts. Makes me wonder why the pastor can't just reach them on *Facebook* or *Twitter*. I'm sure the youth would love to talk to their pastor through that medium."

"I don't know if that's a good idea," Randy said. "But I know for sure that Pastor Ogwoka won't sign on to *Facebook* or *Twitter* to meet the youth there. Maybe years from now. Sweetheart, he is conservative. Conservative pastors don't go on *Facebook* or *Twitter*, they warn against those evil platforms. It will be a while before they see the harmlessness and benefits of *Facebook*, *Twitter* and even *Linkedin*."

"Which is where you and I come in. We can set the stage for a new approach to youth evangelism. If our pastors see that the youth can be effectively reached through the Internet, they will join the ball game. So...are you in?"

Randy said yes and wondered whether Vivian was on *Facebook* or *Twitter*. "When do we start?" he asked.

"We can start with an announcement tomorrow, then take it from there; the sooner the better."

"Can Vivian join us?"

Gosh, Vivian? Kate didn't know what to say. Why did Randy want Vivian on such a holy project? Vivian was a liar, a backstabber; a woman with a shady past and a ceaseless flirt. How was such a woman going to minister to people? Besides, hadn't Randy admitted that a friend who blackmailed another wasn't really a friend? Why was he intent on bringing Viv into the mix?

"You don't like the idea, do you?" Randy asked.

"It's just that...I thought we would make it a family thing." She sighed. "Why Vivian anyway?"

"Have other friends then?"

Kate collapsed on the bed and drew the comforter over her head. It was obvious Randy wasn't into the *Facebook* ministry thing, or why would he bring in a deranged chic he knew just too well she would detest working with? Fuming, Kate said, "Sweetheart, you should've just said no if you didn't want to do it!"

"What? Why do you say that?"

"You knew I would say no to Viv's involvement in this and that my refusal would kill the idea, right?"

Randy said no and wondered why Kate always read conspiracy into everything he said. Getting back to sleep, he said, "What's her other name by the way?"

Kate finally had enough. "Look, if you are interested in that cold gossiper you can go find out what her other name is yourself. But let me warn you—whatever you do with Vivian, nothing can remain sealed forever; sooner or later she will tell me everything."

Randy, tongue-in-cheek, said, "Does that mean your friendship rolls on unperturbed?"

Kate didn't want to talk anymore, but she just couldn't help it. Feeling Randy had deliberately slighted her, she said, "I have a secret I've never told you!"

It worked. Randy drew a deep breath. These secrets couldn't be good for his marriage or health. Wasn't this the kind of stuff that caused depression? What was the tit-for-tat supposed to achieve? Coiling with fear, he finally said, "Kate, I can't handle any more darkness."

"It's not darkness."

"Then what is it?"

"A confession!"

And with that Kate had inadvertently set the stage to drop her most devastating secret yet on Randy.

It was going to change everything.

———

In Muthaiga, Carol, her mother and father looked at everything going on in the various Nairobi bedrooms through a sampler Luciferian Screen in the basement. They saw husbands and wives bickering late into the night then sleep with their back to each other. They saw men and women sleeping in each other's arms in hotels across the city when they should have been with their spouses. They saw female students in the various universities in Nairobi seek solace in the unpredictable embrace of male ones in hostels that were no longer easy to classify as male or female.

In one Nairobi hotel, they even watched with satisfaction as one brazen Luciferian strangled a woman he had lured in there and draw her blood with his bare teeth.

Finally impressed by the night's progress, Carol looked at the two top Luciferian priests and said, "Our agents have captured Nairobi, let's now look at Kisumu."

The man squeezed a button on a remote control and Kisumu spread out on the screen. From one end to the other, they watched as men and women danced, drank, partied and engaged in other acts that Christians called *immoral* while the Luciferians called *acts of defiance*. When Carol had seen this magnificent display for the first time—almost five years ago on the night her dad and mom had picked her up from the village at the border—she had asked who was being defied and the woman had said, "God and the Bible!"

"And such defiance goes on throughout Kenya?" she had asked, stunned.

"Not just Kenya," they had said and walked her through cities in Africa, Asia, the Americas, Europe and as far down as Canberra and Wellington. The Luciferians were on a march all across the globe, they told her with unmitigated pride.

"But why the zeal?" Carol had asked.

"Remnants put it best," the man had said. "They call the battle between the Luciferians and God the conflict of the ages.

A woman they call a co-founder of their church actually penned a volume called *The Great Controversy*. If the world read that book and realized what is at stake for humanity, people would seek God in earnest. Our role, Carol, is to keep the world from reading that book and minimize the impact of the Remnant message. More than any followers of Christ, the Remnants are the most dangerous; they pose the greatest threat to our success. That is the reason we have worked hard to destroy that church.

"We have planted confusion in the ranks and sieved in professors who question the creation story. Our belief is that if the literal creation week falls apart, we destroy the basis for the Sabbath, and if we destroy the basis for the Sabbath, we'll have succeeded in undermining the only lasting covenant God has with modern man. We will have finished Him, buried His agenda forever!"

Carol was stunned. "Finish God?"

The woman had said, "In due course you'll come to understand everything, but in a simplified way let me say that our broadest agenda is to force humanity to doubt God, just like Lucifer did with Adam and Eve in the Garden of Eden.

"The premise is simple—when we go around wrecking havoc in the world, causing earthquakes, tsunamis, vicious civil wars and mass starvation, sooner or later people start to wonder about the goodness and omnipotence of the God of the Bible. Get it?"

"I see," Carol had said.

Five years later, that very Carol had become the most prolific Luciferian of all time. There was only one more assignment she had to undertake before she was elevated into a conjugal partnership with the angel of light. She had to convert

Jerome. But would she succeed when they met in Mombasa in two days?

Or would Jerome's blood finally have to be shed?

TEN

"**V**iv, I'm in a fix."

It was six thirty in the morning. Jerome hadn't slept all night but had not wanted Vivian to know his troubled state of mind. Like most issues in his life, he was always private; never revealed anything to Vivian unless his shoe had shrunk to a point it was really hurting. Fearing he had reached that point this morning, he waited until Vivian was awake and fully dressed for work. And because it was a Friday, she was dressed in a pair of Denim jeans trousers and a v-neck top that spotted flowers and a sizeable picture of a lion and her cabs.

"What's going on?" Vivian asked, concerned about the red eyes shooting into hers.

"There's something I've been meaning to discuss with you, but I've repeatedly put off because I lacked the courage to bring it up."

Vivian told Jerome to sit back on the bed. It was still disheveled and unlike other rooms in the house, it was gonna stay that way until either Vivian or Jerome fixed it; which usually was after two days. The house girl, though she was a heck of a worker, was never allowed into this bedroom. Her duties lay elsewhere in the house.

As soon as Jerome sat, Vivian dropped in next to him and said, "Have you been fired?"

Jerome shook his head. "Nothing like that, Viv."

"Are the businesses doing fine?"

"They are in great shape."

"Then what's the matter?"

There were tears in Jerome's eyes and it was the first time since they got married that Vivian had ever seen him look so scared, so out of it. What in the world was going on?

"Sweetheart?" Vivian was beginning to get scared too. This wasn't the way she wanted her Friday to start. No, Friday was *Furahi* day. And besides, the least she expected was a clear, sober head, not the troubles of a man who may have slept with another woman. "Oh my God, Jerome, AIDS?"

Jerome looked Vivian in the eye and told her to calm down. "Geez, I don't have AIDS, okay?"

"Fine, then I'll just sit here and listen to you."

For the next half an hour Jerome walked Vivian through his secret life in Mombasa. He told her the way Carol had taken him to high profile Luciferian meetings and promised him enormous wealth if he became one of them. He described in numbing detail the buildings, city streets and emerging agenda of the Luciferians. Then, just when Vivian thought she'd heard it all, he dropped the bombshell. "Carol wants me to become a Luciferian too."

"Hold on now," Vivian said sharply. Her eyes were squarely on Jerome's. "She wants you to become a what?"

"A Luciferian."

"Isn't that just a cute way of saying a devil worshipper?"

Jerome hesitated. He'd all along tried to compartmentalize this mater. He'd argued that there was an angle of Luciferianism that was all devil worship and another that was strictly business. It was the business angle that excited him, not devil worship. In fact, when it came to worship, he saw himself as a solid Christian; a man who loved his wife and a strong church member. So ... was it really fair for Vivian to lump all that up as devil worship?

"Why?" Vivian asked.

"Why what?"

"Why would you choose to become a devil worshipper?" she asked, tears forming in her eyes.

He didn't answer.

Back in his humble village church, Jerome's mother was the Head Elder—a position she had held for years. Each morning Jerome heard her pray for all her children, beseeching the Lord to take good care of the boys and girls and keep them from the snares of the devil. He recalled the one evening when sudden strong winds had come through the gate just before his grandpa was buried and threatened to uproot the roof. Where they had gathered, Mama stood up and rebuked the strong winds in the name of Jesus and things became quiet again. That night, stunned by Mama's power over the ghastly winds, Jerome had walked to the lady and asked how she had managed to stop the winds.

"Oh no no, son, I didn't stop the winds," Mama had said. "The Almighty God did!"

"He gave you the power?"

"Here is a little secret—when you call upon the name of the Lord, the evil spirits tremble. Even the faith of a child is sufficient to drive the devil back. I pray you will always remember that."

This morning Jerome remembered Mama's sweet voice, but it was no comfort. Carol was not an evil spirit; she was a smart business woman—and her role in the Luciferian movement wasn't crazy like the folks he had seen strip naked and bow to that scary statue; hers was more of a motherly recruiter. She stayed decent.

"Jerome?"

"Sorry, sweetheart. Here is my dilemma. I'm supposed to meet Carol in Mombasa on Saturday, but I fear that things may go terribly wrong. This time I'm really worried."

"But why?" Vivian asked. "What is she going to do to you that she hasn't done before?"

"Let me put it this way. There is a meeting of the Luciferians in East Africa at the Coast. That meeting takes place every five years and each Luciferian agent is supposed to showcase his or her trophies. Carol is determined to showcase me as a recruit of hers."

"Are you saying Carol is an agent?"

"One of the top ones," Jerome said.

"And if she showcases you, why would that be such a big deal? What would it take from you?"

"My God is what it would take from me. Let me explain—"

It was now 7.30 a.m. and Vivian was supposed to leave for work, but this was just too intriguing to ignore or put off for a later time. As the weaverbirds chirped on the swaying branches of the jacaranda and the children jumped into buses that would bring them to school on time, Vivian took Jerome's hand and led him to the dining room. There, Jerome said, "You gonna have breakfast with me today?"

"Seems like I have no choice. I'm gonna call Kate to let her know I'll be late this morning."

"Won't be in trouble?"

"Nope."

Vivian grabbed the phone and called Kate, then she went ahead and set the breakfast table. While they ate, Jerome explained how the Luciferians worked. "The battle is not about appearances," he stressed between bites. "The war has always been for souls."

"I don't get it," Vivian said.

"Okay, let me bring it home. Have you seen the way Christians carry their Bibles and wear clean clothes to church on Saturdays and Sundays and equate that to holiness? And have you seen the way folks who dress in the best clothes and drive flashy cars come together in little groups that exclude those who don't look as well endowed?"

Vivian crashed a boiled egg and set it between two slices of whole wheat bread to form an appetizing sandwich, then she took a deep bite. She followed it with a gulp of orange juice to wash down the thing. Finally able to talk, she said, "Are you saying those who drive posh cars and dress sharply can't worship in truth and in spirit?"

"Not at all," Jerome said. "But I happen to know, from my chat with Carol, that Luciferians invented outward piety to replace the kind of piety that really matters—*piety of the soul*. In essence, therefore, the Luciferians don't have to fight for your soul if it is not with God. The fact that it is not with God means it is with them. Now ... I know you are wondering what that has to do with Carol and the meeting in Mombasa. Here is the answer. For me to be showcased, I'll have to have been converted and brought fully into the fellowship of global Luciferians. There are a string of rituals I'll have to take under my belt to become a member. It is that serious."

Vivian put her cup down. "But did you say they'll make you rich if you joined them?"

Jerome nodded. "They control all the wealth and power in this world. Dominion is to them!"

"So what will you do?" she asked.

"Vivian, I don't know what to do. My fear is that Carol has told me so much that if I walked away now she'll want to kill me; turn my blood in as a sacrifice to Lucifer!"

"Lucifer? As in Satan?"

Again Jerome hesitated. Ever since he started going around with Carol, he'd never heard anybody refer to Lucifer as Satan. In fact, in the ritzy Mombasa hotel where Carol had shown him pictures of Lucifer, the being had looked like a god. There was nothing scary about him at all. Just looking at him in the album, it felt like Christians maligned the good name and recklessly soiled the image of a celestial being—an angel who controlled the world. It felt so wrong.

"Vivian, I don't want to die!"

Die? Vivian drew a deep breath and exhaled in a slow, deliberate fashion. So her troubles with Kate were nothing but a ride in a Jaguar over a manicured St. Tropez park? "Why and how did you allow yourself to get into a mess like this, honey?"

"Too late for that," Jerome said.

"Okay, then here is what I want us to do. I'm not an expert on spiritual matters or anything like that, but I know that we are at a point only God can help us. We need to go to church right now. Dress up!"

Jerome coiled. "What!?"

Vivian's tears formed and she looked Jerome in the eye to let him see just how scared she was. For years she had desperately wanted to be like her rich sisters, but if wealth came by way of walking away from God, she didn't want any part of it. Losing one's soul to the devil was a bigger sin to her than lesbianism. She worried that Luciferians made the great controversy between good and evil become just too real, too immediate.

Jerome said, "You don't get it, do you?"

"You really want to go to that meeting?" Vivian asked, amazed that her Christian husband would even contemplate such a move after he knew what was at stake.

"Sweetheart, I have no choice," he said.

"You are going?"

Jerome got up and started to put the plates away. He was surprised by how badly Vivian had taken the whole thing. Couldn't she see that all he wanted to do was fool Carol for a while then walk away with wealth and power? Hadn't she always wanted to have a nicer car than her sisters' and a bigger home and a fat bank account and imported Italian clothes and…? How in the world did she expect to have all that stuff without becoming a Luciferian? One thing Christians needed to understand was that nobody became rich without bending to the powers of He who Controls the World!

"I asked if you are going?" Vivian said.

"I am."

Vivian got her bag and car keys and walked toward the door. She said, "Sweetheart, I have a feeling you may be blowing your last chance to remain on the right side of this battle. I know I've had my fair share of failures, even felt at times like I was under the spell of evil forces, but the Lord is gracious; He forgives sinners. Whatever it is you have done in Mombasa in the past, and whatever it is you have done with Carol, God is able to forgive you. He is able to place you on a path to spiritual renewal; just say now that you belong to Him. That's all!"

Jerome shook his head and went back to the bedroom as Vivian walked to the car. The instant the car started, Carol appeared out of nowhere and kissed Jerome on the cheek. "You did well!"

Jerome almost fainted. Carol had never done anything like that before. "How did you get in here?"

"Well, I don't think I've ever told you that as a top Luciferian agent I have power to be anywhere anytime." She smiled. "And by the way, I've seen that Vivian is going to be a problem. Do you want me to finish her for you...for the sake of our cause?"

Jerome froze. "You want to kill my wife?"

"No, Jerome. I don't want to kill your wife. But you need to know this—that anybody who stands in the way of the mission of Luciferians is targeted for elimination. It is my advice that we kill that woman; let her blood flow to Lucifer as a worthy sacrifice from you. If you don't want us to drink her blood now, how about when we come back from Mombasa?"

Jerome couldn't believe it. So this is what Vivian had feared? Worried about where things were going, he looked Carol in the eye and started to talk. But the only word that came out of his mouth was sorry. Before he could say more, a silent, whispering wind made its way through the window and carried Carol away. He watched in amazement as she smiled, then disappeared. It was in that moment that he picked up the phone and dialed Vivian, who was now on her way to meet Pastor Ogwoka at the Remnant Church.

Vivian answered on a second ring. "Are you okay?"

"Viv, wait for me at the office; we must go to that church you talked about right now."

"Okay. I'm actually on my way there right n..." The next thing Jerome heard was the unmistakable sound of a horrific crash.

Carol had killed his wife!

———

Deep in the village, Jerome's mom went on her knees to pray as she did every morning. She prayed for her sons and daughters and even remembered to lift up those who the devil had targeted to destroy. "Lord," she said, "defeat the evil schemes of that ancient deceiver. Don't let him claim victory over the hosts of the Most High!"

It was right in the middle of that intercessory prayer that the Lord of Hosts had sent his angels to form a protective ring around Vivian in Nairobi. The Mercedes Benz that had come speeding along Milimani Road had smashed into her truck and damaged it extensively, but she had walked away with only minor bruises.

Later, when word had reached Jerome's mom about the accident, she had said, "Glory be to God!"

What Jerome had deliberately failed to mention was that Vivian's truck was hit when she was just about to turn left onto the Remnant Church grounds to have a word with the presiding pastor about Satanism. He lacked the nerve to talk.

ELEVEN

Kate was awake by 5:30 a.m. It was usually the time she woke up to help Bill get ready for school. On a good day her morning chores ran right into 6:30, in time for her to beat the bumper-to-bumper traffic on Uhuru Highway. What Kate had never understood was why all the folks who lived this side of town always woke up at about the same time and drove toward the CBD at the same time. The jam such behavior created was thin and long. The funny thing was to see men and women curse and hoot after 7:00 a.m. for being late! Why hadn't they just started early if they were in such a hurry? Did it take a nuclear physicist to figure this out? It just didn't make any sense.

This morning, though, Kate was in no hurry. She had a secret to tell Randy. Matter of fact, over the years she'd wanted to tell Randy the only secret she'd kept from him, but she had never found an opportune moment or a good enough excuse to talk. Last night, however, Randy had given her a reason to. He had pissed her off by repeatedly asking about Vivian. Why was he so interested in Vivian? And why did he ask about Jerome? Did he want to befriend Jerome so he got to Viv?

"Aren't you getting late?" Randy finally asked, surprised by Kate's choreographed slowness.

"I'm the boss," she fired back.

"So bosses can be late at will? Who sets a good example to your workers if you are the one who trashes office rules as you please?"

Kate murmured something through the corner of her mouth, then she said audibly, "There's something I've been meaning to tell you."

"I thought so," Randy said with a cruel smirk. "I knew all along you've been seeing Jerome behind my back."

Kate couldn't believe Randy would repeat such a claim even after she'd disabused him of it last night. She recalled the days they were better friends than now. How could two people who had loved each other through the years come to a point of such low trust? And when were things ever going to get back on track?

"Did you sleep with him?" Randy growled.

"No!"

"Did you kiss him?"

"No!"

"Did you...."

"Shut up, Randy. I've never been interested in that man. He is not my type!"

"Then what in the world do you wanna tell me?"

"Dallas."

Randy, just out of the bathroom and still with a towel around his waist, found the pair of trousers to his pin-stripped, blue Gilberts suit and shoved them on. Next, he put on his V-neck vest and followed it with a maroon silk tie. After looking at himself in the mirror, he slapped on his coat and only then did he say, "Dallas? Can this wait till evening?"

"Why? You don't want to hear what happened in Dallas?"

"Some breaking news you heard? Look, Kate, I don't care about America anymore. Spare me the staleness."

Of course Randy didn't care about America. He still recalled with bitterness the September morning when four FBI agents showed up at his Chicago residence and told him he was under arrest.

"For doing what?" he had asked.

"You've violated the terms of your status in this country. We need you to accompany us," the leader of the team had said.

"Accompany you to—where?"

"We will inform your wife where you are later in the day."

"Fine. Let's go."

But soon what had started as a simple arrest for two Islamic books published by a company Randy owned became an immigration case. Randy was required to show cause why an immigration judge should not order his deportation for engaging in activities that gravely undermined the security of the United States of America. In the coming days Randy was interrogated by FBI agents in Indianapolis, Burlington and Washington D.C. What the Feds wanted to know was whether Randy, through his niche publishing firm, had acted as a conduit for funds transferred by terrorists into and out of Chicago. It was a case of prove us wrong or you are in big trouble.

While at the D.C. offices of the FBI, Randy had befriended an agent who seemed to believe his innocence. He had asked the lady why the U.S. government was treating him like a criminal when all he had done was publish two class texts for a Kenyan Islamic scholar. "Since when did the government here start being so paranoid?"

"Since Osama," Jeaner had said.

Jeaner was a petite blonde, a woman so beautiful that Randy believed she was in the force to entice men to divulge information. A native of Montgomery, Alabama, she was smart, alert and extremely friendly. Unlike the cold boys who crisscrossed the hallways like robots, she had a sunny demeanor and went out of her way to make folks feel human. Something about her was as welcoming as it was intriguing. She was the kind of woman your sixth sense told you to avoid but you just couldn't. She was going to be your downfall because she made you feel loved even though you knew that love within the halls of the FBI offices came with a tagline—*I'll pass on whatever you tell me to my bosses.*

On Randy's seventh day under federal detention, however, he called Jeaner aside and asked what his options were. "Is there any chance this will end soon, Jeaner?"

"Soon meaning?"

"A week? Perhaps two?"

Jeaner shook her head. "As we speak your accounts have been frozen and your company's offices in Chicago have been shut down, pending investigation. What you need to know, though, Randy, is that your company is not the only one affected; there are historical American companies that have been similarly affected by the new policies."

"The **W** policies you mean?"

"Let's call them Homeland Security measures. As things stand now, nobody is in a mood for compromise. Benefit of doubt is no longer a guiding principal here. Truth be told, it will be long till they clear either you or your company. My experience in this department tells me it may take a new administration to lift some of the sweeping policies instituted by the **W** administration."

"So if you were me, Jeaner, what would you do?"

Jeaner knew that Randy had a son and a wife back in Chicago, and that since the business was shut by the Feds, it was only a matter of time before they ran out of funds to support themselves. Chicago was an expensive city. She said, "Randy, I don't want to discourage you in any way since I know you've hired some of the best attorneys to handle this case, but this is one of those times when the best attorneys in the land will do you no good. As a friend I would advise you to leave the States if you can. I know it would be a daunting task to make preparations to exit, but it would be your best option."

"Best, huh?" In that moment, the twenty years Randy had lived in the United States came playing back in rapid succession. He recalled the day he landed in Detroit, his school life in Michigan, his high flying days as the President and CEO of a successful publishing firm, then his humiliating arrest in Chicago. How could life have taken such a dramatic turn without a warning?

"Yes, it's your best option," Jeaner deadpanned.

"Well, say I decided to leave the country without the coercion of a negative ruling, will I then be released from this facility?"

"No," Jeaner said.

"How does it play out?"

"The Feds will ensure you've truly left the States by seeing you off at La Guardia. From La Guardia you'll be in the hands of a Federal Marshall on whatever flight you use right into Europe or wherever. Once in your country, though, you'll be in the hands of your government."

"You really want me to go through that humiliation?" Randy asked Jeaner, looking her in the eye.

"The alternative is worse," she said.

Later that night, Randy had called Jeaner and asked her to inform Kate that life in the United States had come to an end. "Tell her to sell everything and meet me in Nairobi."

Within two weeks of that candid talk with Jeaner, Randy left the United States, hoping the Senator from Illinois, Barack

Obama, would soon become President of the USA and return America to its glory days of the Clinton years. This morning, though, the prospect of President Obama turning America around seemed remote indeed. And while Kate was optimistic about that land and wanted to talk about Dallas, Randy was adamant that America had lost its way and that Obama had done little to reverse the inhumane treatment foreign nationals went through should they run afoul of the law. Even worse, immigrants today faced tougher odds in the States under Obama than they did under W. *Some brother this guy is, man!*

"I can see you are determined not to hear anything about Dallas or America, but this can't wait," Kate finally said, clutching her bag and standing by the door.

"What is it?" Randy said impatiently.

"Remember the time I visited my friend in Dallas?"

"I do." It was so long ago, but Randy remembered the occasion well. He did because he had vehemently objected to the trip but Kate had stubbornly gone.

Kate said, "When I went there I met my childhood boyfriend and went to visit his apartment on a Saturday afternoon."

Randy's jaw dropped. "What!?"

"When I got to his apartment, where he had invited me, I found him with his white girlfriend and the two treated me like trash!"

"Really?"

"It's true!"

But Randy didn't believe her. What Kate didn't know was that two years after that visit, a sister to Kate's childhood boyfriend had called and told Randy everything. All these years

Randy had known Kate's little secret but had played it cool to keep things calm at home.

Amused by Kate's suspicious timing, he finally said, "So, my dearest Kate, why have you chosen to tell me about a ten-year-old indiscretion today?"

Kate glanced at her watch and started walking down the steps while keeping the door open. Once next to the car, she opened the door as she said, "I want us to have no secrets between us, sweetheart."

But again Randy didn't believe her. He knew this was about Vivian. Kate was worried about the sudden interest her husband had in Vivian. This couldn't be good, she feared.

The two might just hook up!

———

Though Kate's intention had been to slap Randy hard with her Dallas story for repeatedly asking about Vivian last night, she'd only ended up making him more furious and probably pushed him more decisively toward the welcoming embrace of that woman. As she eventually rolled into heavy traffic on Uhuru Highway, she felt like her marriage was suddenly propped up courtesy of a thin thread indeed. The question on her mind was—what man could withstand being pummeled with two devastating secrets in one day? Could that be the reason Randy was suddenly interested in Vivian? Worried that Viv might also want to torment her, she dialed Viv's number and waited on the line.

After a fifth ring, though, it was Jerome who answered. "I'm so sorry, Kate. Your friend was involved in a bad accident this morning. She's at the Nairobi Hospital."

Kate felt a sharp jolt. Why were so many weird things happening to her? Fearing that her life was about to turn dark indeed, she called her mama and asked the old lady to pray for her. "The devil is after me," was how she put it. What Kate didn't know was just how accurate her fears were, because though it was true the devil was after her, it was her secret past that was going to be used to finish her. And the big deal was—it wasn't the two secrets she had already revealed to Randy, it was the secret Carol was about to resurrect in her life.

Her three-decade-old Luciferian connection.

TWELVE

Pastor Kevin Ogwoka was the senior pastor of the Remnant Church. Trained at the flagship denominational theological seminary in Berrien Springs, Michigan, he was highly regarded by his conservative congregation that boasted some of the leading professionals in the church; and he had even managed to set in place youth-friendly policies that had drawn the Nairobi youth to the three-thousand-member church. Because of his introduction of a unique blend of the modern and the traditional in worship, he had made the services so lively that the church's youth had no problem attracting and retaining youth from other congregations—even the deeply bored.

The enormously talented Kisii preacher was a short man whose self-deprecating humor sent his adoring congregants into fits of laughter. There were those who faulted him for excessive playfulness behind the pulpit, but even they gave him credit for delivering his sermons with incredible zeal once he got going.

In spite of his choice to be a pastor, having turned down a call to professorship at the Eldoret Campus of the church's flagship institution of higher learning in the eastern Africa region, he was nonetheless regarded as one of the top systematicians in the church and a leading thinker on matters related to civil liberties. On many occasions, when leaders at the Nairobi Synod—the century-old entity that oversaw church work in Kenya—needed a scholar to advise on how to handle budding relations between Christianity and Islam, he was brought in to craft the strategy…and his outside-the-box ideas worked like he had subjected them to experimentation and they had passed the test.

This morning, however, while in his office at the church, his secretary knocked and never waited to be allowed in. Pushing in the peeled back door, the lady said, "Pastor, there's a guest here to see you!"

Pastor Ogwoka had long ago told his dutiful secretary that only important visitors should be accorded such deferential treatment, so judging that whoever was out there fitted the bill, he stood up and held his breath to see who popped through the door. When he saw a lady with a wrapped hand, her plaster seemingly fresh, he was taken aback. He looked at the secretary quizzically, but she just shut the door and left.

Pastor said, looking at the lady, "Have a seat err…?"

"Sorry, I am Vivian."

"Thank you, Vivian."

The pastor's office was not the kind of place you went to find anything ostentatious. Tacked right at the back of the giant church, it boasted a tired swivel chair, a softwood desk and a cabinet that carried a ton of books. On the wall was a giant portrait of Jesus Christ, a white lamb in His gentle hand, and several pictures of members of the church at various functions.

Dropping back into the black chair with a sense of purpose, Pastor Ogwoka looked intently at the woman on the other side of the desk and uttered his words with calculated tentativeness. "Vivian," he said, "what may I do for you this morning?"

"It's a long story, Pastor err…?"

"Sorry. I am Pastor Ogwoka."

"Thank you. Well, Pastor, I'm here because I need help. Allow me to go straight to the point. This past night my husband told me things that have shaken me to the core. He told me about a woman he met in Mombasa. That flashy woman, according to what I could gather, is a devil worshipper, a prominent member of the Luciferian movement. She promised my husband enormous wealth and power if he converted to Luciferianism.

"Now, the reason I'm here this morning is because as we speak, that woman and my husband are finalizing plans to fly to Mombasa tonight. He told me that the Luciferians are going to hold their largest convention ever in that coastal city. The convention is a quinquennium event, but this one promises to be the largest and most significant ever. At that convention, Pastor, my husband is supposed to be paraded as a new convert. I want you to stop him from going!"

"Did you say Luciferians?" Pastor Ogwoka asked.

"That's what they call themselves."

Pastor Ogwoka, an avid reader, had heard of the Luciferians. He knew that Luciferianism was nothing but raw devil worship when all its layers were peeled back. While a pastor in Kisii, many years before going to the States for further studies, he had come into contact with a young woman who collected other girls' hair and nails and sliced her victims with razorblades to draw blood, which she screamed with delight upon seeing. Then there was the boy whose parents had called him to pray for in Nyamira because he had a habit of lapsing into glazed stares and repeating the words Lucifer…Lucifer…Lucifer!

And while in the States, the pastor had at one time strayed into the compound of a church that had a strange signpost by the gate. It said: **The Church of Christian Scientists**. Putting that together with Lyn Cruise's secretive Scientology, free masonry, Sluts for Satan, and other occultist forms, the pastor had realized that devil worship was a global phenomenon.

While in African villages it came in the form of *sangomas* and witches and night runners, in the cities it came in the form of sophisticated, inexplicable money largesse and raw power. And while in sub-Saharan Africa it may have confined itself to less disturbing forms, in the West it was now open and deeply entrenched.

Given what he knew, the pastor didn't appear stunned that the devil worshipers were in Nairobi; what took him aback was that a real human being, a lady who had come into direct contact with a potential Luciferian, was seated in his office. What was he going to do with the suspicious, beautiful woman?

"Pastor Ogwoka," Vivian called in a hushed tone. Her words were calculated to have maximum impact. "They don't call the devil Satan, they insist on calling him Lucifer."

"Not surprised at all. But if I may be a little nosy, would you tell me what happened to your arm?"

"Sure. Sorry I didn't tell you when I walked in. I've just come from Nairobi Hospital. I was involved in a freak accident this morning along Kenyatta Avenue, right next to the Shell at Pan Afric. Do you know that intersection where you dive off Kenyatta Avenue and gun left toward Upper Hill?"

Pastor Ogwoka nodded.

"Right there!"

"What happened?"

"It was a freak accident as I've just said. This sleek Mercedes Benz just shot out of nowhere and slammed into my car full speed. If you saw my car now you won't believe I came out of that mangled wreck alive. It's amazing I'm here talking to you."

"Your husband…where is he? Was he at the hospital with you?"

Vivian nodded. "He was, but I can't tell when he left. I've tried calling him twice, but he won't take my call."

"You offended him?"

"No."

"Did you two argue over something?"

Vivian thought for a sec, then she nodded. "Pastor, of course we argued. Look at the magnitude of the problem we are dealing with here. I pleaded with my husband not to go to Mombasa; when he didn't want to see my point of view, I let words shoot out of my mouth like bullets out of a revolver. I was pissed off."

"So he insists on going?"

"He's dead set. He says if he doesn't the woman may harm him. She may even kill him."

Pastor Ogwoka was in a fix. In all his years in the ministry, he had never dealt with anything like this. Besides, at the seminary his world-renowned professors had focused his attention on history of the church, the writings of Ellen G. White and the post-modernist thought patterns that were increasingly wrecking havoc on *faith* by questioning time-honored biblical stories like creation, the existence of a real David and the Jonah drama. No, no one at the seminary had taught Pastor Ogwoka how to handle sorcery and witchcraft and the more sophisticated form of occultism presenting itself before him this morning.

Swinging on his swivel chair in a nervous mannerism, he said, "Vivian, is it possible to see your husband before he flies out?"

"I'll ask him to see you."

"His name?"

"Jerome."

"I don't want to make any promises, my daughter, but I'm going to pray about this deeply troubling situation. It's the very first time I'm dealing with one of its kind."

Vivian frowned. "Really? How can you say that when Jerome says Luciferians are in every church? He told me, just this morning, that it's because of Luciferians that academic squabbles and philosophical differences rock the church…and lukewarm tendencies have become so pervasive. Pastor Ogwoka, I don't mean to alarm you, but it helps to be aware that the Luciferians are in this church just as they are in every church. In fact, according to Jerome, your church is especially targeted by Luciferians because they say the **Remnant Church of God** is the church that has the **Truth**. He says that if the believers got their act together and spread the gospel of Jesus Christ in accordance with the revelation Christ imparted, the world of Luciferians would be turned upside down. Luciferian agents fear the Remnant Church!"

"Is that why you came to me?" Pastor Ogwoka asked.

"Partly yes, Pastor. I live right up here on Milimani Road. Kiwi Apartments. I've seen this church whenever I drive by, but I've never bothered to worship or find out what goes on here. My husband, who is a Remnant believer, by the way, has asked me time and again to come here with him, but I've always declined. I was raised nominal."

"Wait. Your husband comes to church here?"

"No. He goes to a church called Karen, wherever that is. I've never accompanied him there. By the way, with everything going on I've got to ask—is there really a church like that?"

Pastor Ogwoka smiled. "The Lord's remnant church is large and is probably the fastest growing movement in Kenya. We have churches in Nairobi, Nakuru, Kisumu, Mombasa,

Eldoret and some of the remotest places in Kenya. In fact, I have friends who say that all around the world there are two things you won't miss wherever you go—Remnants and Coca cola."

"Really? So *Remnantism* is global?"

"We have our headquarters in the United States, Maryland. The large white building you saw to your left when you came in here is the headquarters of the Remnants in Kenya. Then we have the movement's regional headquarters up a beautiful hill."

"Regional?"

"Yes. It's like this—the regional office oversees work in Kenya, Uganda, Tanzania, Ethiopia, Somalia, Rwanda, Burundi and the DR Congo and South Sudan. But let me not bore you with the structure of our church; it gets complicated. Still, I must extend a hand of welcome to you. Whenever you have time, come fellowship with us."

"I will."

"I'm looking forward to seeing you here. Before you go, let us pray. Can we?"

The pastor prayed. When he was done, he saw Vivian out. It was while he stood by the door that the name Jerome first rang a bell. Could he be the guy he bought his Toyota Caldina from a little over a year ago? Wasn't the guy's name Jerome? Was this young woman his wife? If she was, Pastor Ogwoka was going to do everything to save this troubled family; and there was only one way to do it.

Take the dragon head-on.

———

It wasn't until 12:30 p.m. that Jerome finally took Vivian's call. When he did, Vivian cut to the chase. "Look, Jerome, Pastor Ogwoka wants to see you urgently."

Jerome didn't talk.

"Did you hear me, Jerome? Pastor Ogwoka is waiting for you at the church. You must hurry."

"Which church?"

"The big one on Milimani."

Jerome couldn't believe Vivian had gone to the pastor. This was the reason he had left her at the hospital in the first place—because he had feared she would want him to come along. So she had gone?

Vivian said, "Still going to Mombasa?"

Jerome didn't answer that either. He cut the line and refused to take Vivian's subsequent calls.

He was so mad!

***

Over in leafy Muthaiga, Carol followed Pastor Ogwoka and Vivian's conversation with keenness on her wide screen. She was amazed to hear the things Vivian was telling the pastor. As a good friend she was going to ask Jerome to sacrifice that woman, let her blood flow to the bottom of the Indian Ocean, or Carol would just have to do it herself.

Vivian was just too dangerous to keep on this side.

THIRTEEN

Pastor Ogwoka got home at 4:30 p.m. Today he hadn't even had lunch. Not that he hadn't gone, it's just that when he had gone down to Veggie Cuisine—the popular vegetarian restaurant run by the church opposite Integrity Centre, on Milimani Road—he had had no ounce of appetite left. Even though he had tried to deny it, Vivian's visit had shaken him to the core. The words that had kept ringing in his mind were:

The Luciferians are targeting your church
There are many Luciferians in your congregation

Then at 1:30 p.m., having waited for Jerome to call for hours, he had gotten up and walked down to the restaurant. Like usual, it was neat and the food mouth-watering. From the vegetarian meatballs to the fried kales to the *magira* and sweet potatoes and finally to the *kienyeji nyoyo*. This restaurant was in a class of its own. And the staff were welcoming and friendly. If ever there was a group of people who wore Christ on their sleeve as they served and interacted with God's children, it was these guys. They were truly a people of God.

Today, though, a leading minister was a deeply worried man. So worried was Pastor Ogwoka that when Rose, one of the smiley affable waitresses, approached to take his order he didn't know what to say. He was blank. He seemed incoherent and absent-minded. And later, when two other pastors joined him at the table, he seemed so distant that one of them had to ask whether he was okay or not.

He didn't talk.

Leaving the stunned colleagues at the table, Pastor Ogwoka had gone back to his office and prayed. There, he had pleaded with God for a sense of direction on this matter. He was on his knees for nearly ten minutes, until a persistent call eventually interrupted his tête-à-tête with the Lord. Hoping it was Jerome he had expectantly said, "This is Pastor Ogwoka, Jerome. How may I help you?"

"Pastor Ogwoka, I'm not Jerome. My name is Carol."

"Carol? I'm sorry, have we met?"

"Don't think so."

"Well, what may I do for you?"

Carol hesitated. She wanted her words to come out in a fashion that ejected them with the force of a volcanic eruption. Since it was the first time she was gonna be talking to this pastor, in spite of visiting his church many times before, she wanted her subtle entry into the picture to leave no doubt about the magnitude of the danger she posed. This had to be carefully choreographed. Finally ready, she said, "Pastor Ogwoka, a friend of mine was supposed to have called you, but he is unable to. He asked me to call on his behalf and pass on his apologies."

"Is it Jerome you're talking about?"

"Indeed, Pastor."

"I see. I would have loved to talk to him before his departure for Mombasa, though. Do you have his phone number?"

Carol thought for a sec, then said yes. She wanted to know what the man of God had up his sleeve; how he intended to deal with the matter. She said she was gonna text the number pronto, then she hung up. She sent the number. A minute later, Pastor Ogwoka called Jerome and cut to the chase. "Two things," he started. "First, could you be the same Jerome who sold me a Toyota Caldina a year ago?"

Jerome was taken aback. Over the past two years he had sold too many cars to keep track of whom he'd sold what. But one thing he knew for sure was that he rarely sold Caldinas or any such lowly brands. His stock included Prados, Highlanders, Harriers, BMWs, Benzes and Volvos. If at all he had sold a Caldina he must have disposed of it for a friend. But not to sound disrespectful, he said, "It may well be that I sold you a Caldina, Pastor Ogwoka."

"It was blue."

"Oh wait, was it a station wagon?"

"No, a saloon."

"Hhmm, I can't quite recall that car, but I wouldn't be surprised if it turned out you bought it from me. My bazaar is out in Hurlingham."

"Aha—?"

"It's called Mercury Cars Ltd."

"That's it," Pastor Ogwoka said. "You sold me a beautiful car. It has served me very well."

"I'm glad."

"But that's just one of the reasons I called—to thank you for that service. The second reason I called is to discuss a matter that has your dear wife deeply concerned. I would have loved to discuss these matters face-to-face, but your friend, Carol, has called and told me you can't make it here."

Jerome stammered, then he kept quiet.

"Since you can't make it here now, there's just one thing I can tell you right away. Are you listening?"

"I am, my pastor."

"Don't go to Mombasa with that woman!"

"Vivian told you I was going with Carol?"

Carol? Pastor's voice suddenly turned wry and his lips twitched, a nervous habit that set in whenever he was agitated or badly shaken by something. What had him in a panic mode was that name. **Carol**. If it was true it was Carol he had talked to…was Jerome saying the pastor of the top church in the country had talked to a Luciferian? So it was the Luciferian who was keeping Jerome from meeting him? Wasn't this a classic case of the Great Controversy, just as Ellen G. White saw it play out between God and Satan after the fall of Lucifer? Wasn't this evidence that Satan had upped his game and was now coming directly after the elect of the Lord? What he couldn't understand was why the Lord had thrust him in the role of a commander for the hosts of heaven. Was he gonna be strong enough to go toe-to-toe with that ancient prince of darkness? Was he going to slay the dragon?

With finality, after a brief prayer, Pastor Ogwoka said, "Jerome, the Lord loves you. As one called to lead His children from the alluring snares of the devil, I ask you not to go to Mombasa. Don't leave Nairobi with Carol. When you leave your office this evening, go home to your dear wife, Vivian. She needs you!"

"But, Pastor, do you understand the danger I am in?"

"I do."

"And do you understand that the Luciferians don't take no for an answer?"

"I do."

"Then you must understand that if I don't go to Mombasa you may have no Jerome to talk to tomorrow."

Pastor Ogwoka drew the phone from his ear and wondered what he should tell the troubled young man. He realized that Jerome was in a deep fix. But was there any sense in living a life devoted to Satan and miss eternal life? Deciding it was better for the boy to die in Christ rather than live a life devoted to Luciferianism, he said, "Jerome, I beseech you—call Carol right now and tell her you are not going to Mombasa."

"I want to, Pastor, but I'm so afraid."

"Afraid of her?"

"No, of death."

"I was told you are a member of Karen...is that true?" Pastor Ogwoka asked. He was no longer in a mood to plead. He knew that he had just but a short time to save Jerome or surrender the young soul to eternal damnation.

"Pastor, it's true I go to Karen," Jerome said.

"Are you a baptized member?"

"I am."

"Then I believe before you got baptized your pastor told you it does a man no good to gain the world but lose his soul?"

"I was told that, yes."

"Then heed your pastor's warning."

"And if I die?"

The line suddenly cut before Pastor Ogwoka could answer. He tried several times to redial, but it remained silent like a ghostly *gunda*. Fearing it may have been Carol who disrupted the conversation, he called her, but she too didn't bother to answer.

It was after that phone conversation with Jerome that Pastor Ogwoka had gone to Veggie Cuisine to have a bite, but had failed to eat. His mind was preoccupied.

Then later that chilly evening—arriving home at 4:30— he went straight to the bedroom and prayed for Jerome, for Vivian and for his church family. After the fervent prayer, he came to the dining room, where he grabbed a glass and filled it with orange juice. Done, he went to the living room and dropped his weight into one of the two loveseats. As the complaining seat sank with him, he wondered whether he was getting too fat for his challenged height. Did he need to urgently enroll for fitness exercises at BLC?

The phone rang.

"It's Vivian," the caller said when he answered.

But it wasn't really Vivian. It was Carol. Carol wanted to trick the pastor into thinking it was Vivian who had called, and even set up things in a way that made Vivian seem like she was coming on to the pastor. Carol had done such things before and succeeded. This was another chance to set up a mighty preacher.

Pastor Ogwoka, excited to hear from the distressed woman, said, "Vivian, is Jerome home yet?"

"No, Pastor, he's not. But look—I just felt this overwhelming urge to talk to you. Can you call me back right away?"

"Of course!"

"Then call me on my other number. Here it is."

The pastor noted the number Carol just gave him, then dialed it right away. When it was answered, Pastor Ogwoka said, "That was fast. It seems like *Airtel* and *Safaricom* are no longer at war, huh?"

"Who is this?"

"It's Pastor Ogwoka, Vivian. Isn't this the number you just gave me to call you on?"

"Sure," Vivian said, coming up to speed with what she thought was the pastor's first attempt at hitting on her. She was sure she hadn't given the pastor her number and neither had they talked since morning, when she had visited him at his church office; so the only reason he could pretend Vivian had called him was because he wanted a way to start something without looking bad, right?

"Is Jerome home?" the pastor asked.

"Pastor, I'm so glad you called. I was just longing to talk to you too. Actually, I'm on my way home as we speak. Hope I can persuade Jerome not to fly to the Coast."

"I tried earlier; didn't seem like he was inclined to heed my warning."

"He maintained his stubbornness, didn't he?" she fumed.

"I fear that's an accurate assessment of his stance then, but more than that … what bothered me was the fact that the line cut as we talked. We didn't get to finalize things."

"Should've called him back," Vivian said.

"I tried. He didn't answer."

"Then maybe his mind is made up."

"Could be. Anyway, what did you have in mind?"

Pastor Ogwoka was taken aback. Why was Vivian asking him that? She was the one who had called him, right? Why call then ask what he was up to? Was that the latest trick? With an even voice, he said, "But you are the one who called me, Vivian!"

"You called me first," she fired back. Then sensing the futility of engaging the pastor along such a path, she smiled knowingly. Yes, the pastor wanted to flirt. But was it really a good idea to flirt with a man of God? And just why were men like this? Only moments ago she'd been with Randy at Rock Hotel and he'd made it clear he was gunning for a steamy affair. He'd even suggested they go to Wonderland, but she'd declined.

She'd said she wanted God in her life, not an affair with her boss' husband.

Now it was the pastor! Goodness!

Vivian said, "Pastor, do you want us to meet somewhere to talk about this Luciferian thing?"

The pastor was again taken aback by the frontal nature of Vivian's words. He knew that Vivian was hurting and was vulnerable and needed a man to cry on his shoulder, but he wasn't that man. He couldn't be that man. He had to find a way of redirecting her to her husband. That was the more reason Jerome had to stay in Nairobi with his wife, not abandon her in her hour of fear.

"Pastor, can we meet?" she asked again.

"My office perhaps?"

"Sure…or any place better than that."

"Veggie Cuisine?"

Vivian thought for a second. Veggie Cuisine? She'd never heard of it. "Where is that?"

"Right here. On this compound."

"For a start fine," Vivian said.

For a start? What does for a start mean? Pastor Ogwoka played the words in his mind forward, then backward. This was interesting. Stunned by Vivian's growing boldness, he said, "I could make myself available tomorr… Oh wait. Tomorrow is a Sabbath. Can we meet in my office on Sunday?"

"Fine. What time?"

"Ten?"

"Night or day?"

The pastor now stammered. If he had needed any proof that Vivian's intentions were less than noble, there it was. But he wasn't gonna flee just yet. He was gonna take on the devil and whip his butt right in his own turf … in the name of Jesus. After all, wasn't Vivian suddenly behaving just like the Luciferians? What was the difference?

"Pastor, I said night or day?"

"Day of course!"

"Too bad; night would have been a lot more exciting. Just so you know—you can call me any time you feel like talking, okay?"

"I'll consider that. Have a good evening, Vivian."

"Call me Viv."

"Okay, Viv. Talk later."

When Pastor Ogwoka hung up, he shook his head in disbelief. He'd heard mesmerizing tales about Nairobi women and their legendary boldness, but he had never imagined they could be this dangerous. What chance did a man have against the determined advances of a pretty woman like Vivian? What would keep the men in his church from going after a woman of Vivian's seductive skills?

This was the Armageddon!

———

From her screen in Muthaiga, Carol watched with satisfaction as a date was made between Pastor Ogwoka and Vivian. She felt it was better to finish the pastor by hitting him with a major scandal than by trapping his decapitated body in a mangled wreck on Uhuru Highway. In any case, wouldn't it be better to show Ogwoka's dangerous church in negative light before the world than kill him off right away?

And actually, hadn't the trip to Mombasa presented her a perfect opportunity to kill three birds with one stone? This was her chance to turn Jerome into a solid Luciferian, Vivian into a pastor slayer and the church into a laughing stock.

Wasn't this the stuff of Luciferian ingenuity?

FOURTEEN

The final call came at 6:30 p.m. It was Pastor Ogwoka calling to try one last time to keep Jerome from flying to Mombasa with Carol. Over the past few hours he had agonized about whether to try to keep Jerome in Nairobi or not. And since scheduling that appointment with Vivian on Sunday, he had spent most of his time mulling whether he had inadvertently gotten himself into a date with a Luciferian or not. He had further wondered whether Jerome's absence would make it easier for Vivian to reveal stuff about her links to the underworld or make her come on to him with even more boldness and determination.

"Jerome, this is Pastor Ogwoka," the pastor said when Jerome answered the call.

"Yes, Pastor. What may I do for you?"

"Still traveling?"

"Yes."

"In spite of what we know now about the Luciferians and their evil schemes to defeat God's work in Kenya and throughout the world?"

"Pastor, like I told you earlier, I don't see that I really have a choice, do I? Either way I'm gonna die!"

"What do you mean by that?"

Jerome swallowed hard. Bickering with a man of God was not anything he relished. His mama had taught him never to be hard on pastors and other representatives of God on this earth—especially those who were ordained. Besides, hadn't he shoved his neck into a tight noose already? The last thing he wanted was to make things even dicier. So he said, "Pastor, if I survive Mombasa I'll walk away from the Luciferians. But going I must. Or I die tonight!" *Click!*

"Jerome! Jerome!"

But Jerome was gone. Pastor Ogwoka looked at the phone with tears in his eyes and held his chest as if a dagger had just been driven between the ribs. He was hit by a biting sense of loss, a fear that there was nothing more he could do to save Jerome. But more than anything else, he was suddenly worried that he wasn't sitting pretty either. It occurred to him that maybe there was a grand scheme by the Luciferians to bring him down—using Vivian.

The Ogwokas lived in Hurlingham, on Jabavu Lane. His wife, a teacher at a church-run preparatory school, was a down-to-earth lover of the Lord. A staunch believer in the vision and mission of her church and the superiority of its theology and purpose, she always believed that God would never let anything come the way of her family that the family could not handle.

Born into a family of scrounging peasants in the Keroka area, Bosibori Ogwoka went to a local primary school, then to Parapanda High School, where she first came into contact with *Remnantism*. When she joined the Christian school, her father warned her never to convert to *Remnantism*. He said she was in Parapanda for one reason only—to get an education so she could support her own family in the future. Her stern mother had gone even further. She told young Bosibori to work toward becoming Kisii's first woman pilot.

Bosibori had gone to Parapanda and taken in all the learning the Remnants had to offer. At the same time, though, she had also absorbed enough Christian teachings to stir her young mind. One day, when she was in Form III, a pastor came in from Nairobi to conduct a Week of Prayer. The man of God made it plain why anybody who wanted success in this world—and in the world to come—needed to surrender to God. Bosibori took it all in. When the pastor eventually made a call, at the end of that spiritual revival week, Bosibori accepted the Lord Jesus Christ as her personal savior.

But that was just the beginning. In the coming years she dealt with threats from her father and mother and eventually had to flee home to live with a more accommodating aunty in Kisumu. That aunty paid her school fees and even paid for her training as a teacher at Parapanda Teachers College. It was while training in that institution that Pastor Ogwoka met her. Her friends, to this day, insist meeting the young pastor was a chance encounter, but the couple thought those very friends had found a clever way of bringing them together.

From the time they met, Pastor Ogwoka knew he had met his future wife, but Bosibori hadn't been so sure. Her doubts had nothing to do with the man though; they had everything to do with her hard-stance parents. She didn't see how she could ever introduce a Remnant pastor to a father and mother who hated Remnants. Besides, now that she had become a teacher rather than a pilot and had fled home in the face of pressure from the unyielding parents, would those same parents turn around and accept her, leave alone the man?

But tonight that protracted history was the last thing on Pastor Ogwoka's mind. As soon as Bosibori opened the living room door and saw the wrinkles on his face, she knew something had gone awfully wrong. Her husband was troubled.

Pastor Ogwoka tried to hide it. "Welcome home, sweetheart," he said. It was as lifeless a gesture as she could ever remember, but she was gonna play along for now.

Then she saw the phone in his hand. Assessing the situation, she quickly realized that the phone had just delivered some bad news. Steeling herself, she asked her husband what the problem was without uttering a word. It was one of those things that happened after a man and woman had lived together for years and learnt each other well. But rather than the pastor answer, he said, "How was school?"

"The usual."

He bit his lip. "The usual? What's that supposed to mean?"

"It was okay. And how was church?" That was Bosibori. Always quick. Always discerning. Always direct. A thrifty dresser, she saw herself as the controller of the home; the one who brought serenity to a family blessed with rambunctious sons and a lovely, quiet daughter.

The pastor said, "Sweetheart, church was tough today!"

"Politics…or was it something worse?"

"The devil."

"The devil, huh? Don't we deal with that old rascal daily?"

Pastor Ogwoka held her hand and led her to a seat. The living room was sizable and was neatly arranged. Like any good Christian family, the Ogwokas had a couple of Bibles on their coffee table and two or three Remnant hymnals. On the walls they had pictures that revealed the long journey the family had been through over the years. Then there was one large portrait of Christ, a wide smile on His face, His arms outstretched in an inviting gesture.

Bosibori and the girl had always wanted a floor rug to take care of a floor they found rather dull, but so far the pastor and the boys had shot down that suggestion, fearing the rug would cause their noses to run. They were allergic to dust mite.

"Bosibori," the pastor said. "I'm talking about Satan!"

"I know."

"No, you don't."

"I don't know Satan?"

"No, sweetheart."

"Then tell me about him."

"Honey, he came in person!"

"The devil?"

"Yes!"

Bosibori finally sat. "The devil came to church?"

The pastor sat next to her and took her hand. This was how it always happened whenever things were tight at home. After he cleared his throat, the man of God walked his stunned wife through his day, narrating in painful detail how Vivian had come to the office, how she had called later in the day to talk, and how Jerome had just decided he was on his way to attend a Luciferian meeting in Mombasa. "What worries me now," he said, "is that I may be the target of a major plot by the forces of darkness. They want to finish me!"

Bosibori kept quiet.

"My fear is—I don't know what Carol and Jerome will do when they come from Mombasa feeling empowered by the underworld to go after those who call on the name of the Lord."

"You think they'll target you?"

"That's what Vivian says. According to her, the Remnant Church is a target of the Luciferians because we have the everlasting gospel and the drive to bring it to a hurting world. The Luciferians are worried about the work we've done in Nairobi and towns across Kenya. More than that, though, they fear that should our message reach the world and should the Holy Spirit lead church members to live by the tenets of the Scriptures, the Luciferians will be defeated." He paused and drew a deep breath, then exhaling in a staggered fashion he added, "Sweetheart, this is *The Great Controversy* playing out right before us."

"And where is this girl?"

"Vivian?"

"Yes."

"She lives on Milimani Road. Kiwi Apartments."

"As I understand it, you still don't know whether she is clean or tainted, right?"

The pastor nodded.

"Then is it possible for you to walk away from her while you still have a chance?"

Pastor Ogwoka thought for a second, then said, "You want me to just walk away like that? Look, if she is a genuine child of God who is seeking help ... don't you think it wouldn't be right to just shut her out? Would that be the Christian thing to do?"

"No."

"But—?"

"I have a bad feeling about her."

Pastor Ogwoka hated to admit it, but in the past, whenever his wife had warned him about a situation, things had gone terribly wrong if he had ignored her counsel.

"So...what will you do?" Bosibori asked.

The man stood up. "I don't know. I want to pray over this matter and give it some thought at least. By tomorrow night I'll have gotten direction from God."

"And when do those two come back?"

"Carol and Jerome?"

Bosibori looked at her husband in disbelief. Did he realize that Carol and Jerome, those two names, were as good as saying SATAN? Was he aware Satan had come to him in the form of an unpretentious car salesman, a rich Muthaiga woman and a Vivian who he thought was so harmless yet might be the one chosen to trap him?

"You mean Carol and Jerome?" Pastor repeated.

"The devil, yes."

"They come back on Sunday, probably evening."

"Is that when trouble starts for us?"

Pastor Ogwoka drew a deep breath. He knew his wife was right, but he had never handled a situation of this nature. What if Bosibori was wrong this time? What if he was the one who was right for once? He said, "Everything will depend on how we handle this situation. Will you pray for me? Will you stand by me?"

She nodded. "Praying I will. And of course I'll stand by you. But I have a hunch you've been in contact with high profile Luciferians and they won't stop till they have destroyed you and soiled the name of the church with cooked propaganda. My word is—don't have anything to do with Vivian, but if you must, be extremely careful."

"I'll be careful," he said.

Later that evening, right around eight o'clock, Vivian called and told Pastor Ogwoka that Carol and Jerome had just flown out. "They are gone till Sunday," she added as if she hadn't told the pastor that.

"We tried our best," Pastor Ogwoka said. "We can only pray for him now. That's all."

"I know. Have a wonderful night."

"You too." *Click.*

Bosibori watched and listened as the two spoke and a certain fear descended upon her. She knew instinctively that her husband, at the very least, found this Vivian woman pretty fascinating. Didn't he?

Hhmm… This couldn't be good!

———

The flight to Mombasa didn't take long; just an hour thirty minutes. In that time, Carol walked Jerome through expectations. "When we get to Mombasa," she said, "we will stay in the same room."

"Really? Why?"

"Because I want you to be acclimatized."

"Meaning?"

"Meaning I want you to see how the world of Luciferianism works. I want you to watch Kenya, Uganda, Tanzania and the rest of the world. By the time you are done watching what I'll show you, you'll sense that as things stand now, Luciferians have conquered the world. We are firmly in control!"

"And just how will I see that?"

"I have another LS in my room."

"An LS?"

"A Luciferian Screen, just like the one I have in Nairobi. Only a few of us have those. Remember the screen you and I looked at when Vivian and the pastor made their date earlier?"

Jerome exhaled slowly. "Carol, are you sure this stuff is for a weakling like me? Aren't you making a big mistake bringing me along on such a sensitive trip?"

"I wouldn't have brought you along if I thought for a second you couldn't handle it."

"So you want me to be a Luciferian?"

"I need you, Jerome."

"Well, how long will it be till I reach where you are?"

"You mean a knight?"

Carol explained the rankings and warned that there were only seven knights around the world.

"Are you one of them?" Jerome asked.

Carol hesitated. There were certain things she couldn't tell a person who hadn't been initiated yet. Shrugging, she said, "Listen, how about I tell you that tomorrow night?"

"Why not now?"

"Because I care for you!"

Jerome was tense, but he managed a forced smile. He could tell Carol had big plans for him. What he didn't know was what it would take to get to where Carol wanted him to go. Would it take money? Pain? Sex? Or was he gonna have to pay with his own blood?

"Jerome?"

"Yes—?"

"You will be one of the greatest!"

"You think so?"

"I feel it in my bone!"

From that point on, Jerome didn't talk until the Kenya Airways jet bringing them to Mombasa descended on the picturesque coastal city and came to a gliding halt at the Moi

International Airport. Once down and at the airport's lobby, he finally talked. He said, "Carol, I trust you not to harm me."

Carol laughed. "I never would."

But Jerome feared he was fast approaching a point of no return. In the next few hours he was going to face another baptism; only it wouldn't be like the Remnant one—by immersion.

It would be a baptism that sealed his fate. Forever!

FIFTEEN

"**W**ere you with Vivian?"

Kate's question took Randy by surprise. He had just arrived home and found Kate seated in the living room watching a rerun of Oprah. Of all her favorite shows, Oprah was at the top. Many times she left work a little early to make it home just in time to catch the popular show, which regularly started at 6:30 p.m. on Kenya's most authoritative TV channel—KTN.

Today she had come home early, but for a different reason. She was home to confront her husband about Vivian. She had to take control of this situation or things would spiral out of shape very soon.

"You are home early," she said the minute Randy pushed back the door and stepped in.

"That's not righ…" He looked at his watch. "…I guess you're right. But so are you."

"It's my usual time," she said.

"Used to be."

"Huh?"

"Let me tell you a story, Kate. Once upon a time there used to be a loving wife. She worked at an office in Upper Hill. Though truly gifted as a layout editor and loved her books like they were a child, she loved her husband and son even more and made it home early each evening to make them mouth-watering dinner. Her husband loved her enormously and her son adored her and was so protective of her.

"One day, though, that loving wife fell in love with another woman and started revealing one secret after another of past dalliances including a tryst in Dallas. So shocked was the husband that he tried to do something silly…"

"Stop," Kate cut in and turned off the TV and got off the couch. "What did the husband do?"

"He did something he's never done in years."

"What?"

Randy took off his coat and loosened his tie. He was stunned by the way Kate had gotten into the story. He couldn't remember another time when his distracted wife had jumped ears and eyes into a story like she had done just now. But he couldn't talk yet about his day; Kate was still demanding rather than pleading. For heaven's sake, it was him who had the upper hand now not her; couldn't she see that?

"What?" she repeated.

"Nothing." He shrugged. "Forget I said anything."

"Oh, sweetheart, don't treat me like that now. How can you start telling me a story then just stop?"

"What good will it do if I told you?"

"I'll learn something from it."

"Like?"

"How to treat *my* husband."

Randy took Kate's hand and led her to the bedroom. He asked her to stand with him by the wide window. At this hour, the bright-feathered sparrows were scrambling to get home to their little ones in the nests and the bright street lights were just turning on, causing a sudden flash of brilliance in the neighborhood as if city fathers were determined to keep daylight going on unperturbed by something as mundane as time. In the past, the window was a romantic place where they stood when it rained to listen to the soft tap taps of drizzles and watch as young couples cuddled under the glare of the street lights.

And it was by this same window that some of the most intimate things were shared between them; and some deeply painful things revealed. As Randy asked her to observe a giant nocturnal moth flying just underneath a flickering lamp, he said, "Kate, you've dropped two devastating secrets on me in the last few hours. I can only hope there's no third one because I can't take another."

Kate looked down. "I'm so sorry for causing you pain."

"But what hurts me is not the secrets in and of themselves; what I can't understand is that you didn't bother to reveal them while we stood here...by our window earlier. Do you know what that tells me?"

Kate shook her head.

"It tells me that while you and I think we are happily married, our marriage has slipped; the romance is gone; the glue that once caused us to jell has dried and lost its effectiveness. Like many couples, our union has now become a marriage of convenience. We are here for no reason other than to pay Bill's school fees, feed him and raise him in the fear of the Lord." His eyes welled up. "So...what happens to us when the boy is grown and gone? Will we still find a credible rationale for the continued existence of our marriage?"

Kate's tears formed. Randy's words were too harsh. She wanted to lash out, accuse him of seeing a pile of cow dung where there was nothing but a beautiful spread of the brightest midnight roses. It was a defense mechanism that had worked in the past, but this evening Randy's words had touched a raw nerve. Whichever way she looked at it, it was obvious the ambers of love that once drove her to call Randy several times a day, goad her to text him, had burned out. What was now left was the coldness of pretence, the desire to make it seem as if things were okay between them when they both knew they were stuck with dead weight that should have been hurled into the trash heap of broken promises a long time ago. But had this whole thing really started with Vivian? Was she really the one to blame?

"A credible rationale?" Kate asked and it pained her as each of those three words flew off her lips.

"Would you love to be stuck in a loveless marriage?"

"No."

"Tell me then—what's the best way forward?"

Kate wiped a tear. "I'm the one who has caused the pain and led this union to falter. The dark burdens of my past have weighed heavily on us even though I kept them from you." Her tears crawled south freely now. "Can I ask you a question, though?"

On a sigh, Randy said, "Sure."

"Would you have loved it better if I'd kept the secrets from you or are you happier I talked?"

"You know…what I can't understand even now is why you've been deliberately trying to make me the bad guy. Let us go back to the beginning. Do you realize that you only told me about you and Viv because I caught two racy texts between you two? Seems to me like after you confessed you felt you had made a mistake and so rather than seek genuine forgiveness, you sought instead to stoke my jealousy, fearing that I had asked about Vivian with an intention to avenge what you had done to me, right?"

Kate didn't answer.

"Well, can I also ask you a question?"

Kate flinched and guarded herself. She didn't want to have to bear more burden than she already had. Looking at Randy with pleading eyes, she said, "Okay, ask."

Randy cut to the chase. "Is there a third secret?"

A third secret? Kate couldn't answer that right now. She didn't want to lie again. But surely, who knew the secrets that resided deep in the valleys of his/her life without digging methodically to drench them up? And besides, she hated that by not answering the question right away it seemed as though she was hiding something.

"Tell me the truth," Randy urged.

But what was the truth? That Vivian had confided in her she uses love potion to trap women, and that unfortunately the thing traps men too? Or that she suspected Jerome had a thing for her but had never made his move for fear that Vivian would kill him?

"The truth is all I want, darling," he pressed, aware the pressure on Kate was intense and adding.

"As God is my witness, right now, as I stand here next to you, I have no other secret." She looked down in characteristic fashion, then brought her eyes back like a child who had just discovered the world's biggest secret. Finding Randy's eyes, she said, "Do you?"

Randy smiled. That was vintage Kate. She had recovered from Randy's relentless questioning and swiftly turned tables. "Do I have a secret, you mean?"

"Yes—?"

"When I walked in here a while back you asked me if I was with Vivian, didn't you?"

"I did."

"Yes, I was with her."

Kate sighed but didn't talk.

"We met at Rock Hotel," Randy added.

"Why?"

"Two reasons. One, I wanted to find out what drew two beautiful women into lesbianism. I find it incomprehensible that two attractive women would slide into an affair with each other. But the main reason I met Vivian was because I wanted to revenge. I wanted to stoke your jealousy; feel the thrill that drew you into the arms of that woman."

"Were you with her the whole day?"

"Nope."

"Then where was she in the morning?"

Randy was stunned that Kate hadn't heard of Vivian's accident. Had their fallout been that decisive?

"Randy, I'm asking because Viv was not…"

Randy had to cut in. "Sweetheart, Vivian was involved in a nasty accident this morning. She nearly got killed."

"Huh?"

"It was a Mercedes Benz. It came out of nowhere and slammed full throttle into her car. That time you thought she was with me, she was actually in the hospital."

"My God!"

"Some friend you are!"

Don't care what you say. Kate brushed that stinging broadside off and refocused on her newfound line of attack. "So you met her after that accident?"

"Yes."

"After the hospital?"

"Yes."

"She was well enough to meet you?'

"Yes."

Kate's eyes rolled slowly in their sockets. She found the story incredulous and wasn't afraid to let her eyes communicate the sentiments of her heart. She tried hard to avoid talking, but eventually gave it up as she finally let it rip. "Can you blame me, Randy, if I find your story too good to be true? Do you expect anybody with a brain to believe a person involved in an accident this morning left the hospital and met a boyfriend at Rock Hotel? Can that be true?"

Randy laughed at the venom. He knew Kate didn't trust him at this point and was fearful of his intentions with Vivian. Regardless, he had to talk, and his words were not sanitized. "Look, Kate, had I not seen Vivian's state after that accident I wouldn't have believed if someone had told me the story either."

"Fine. Then tell me what she said."

Randy told Kate everything, but kept the fact that Vivian had turned down his advances to himself. He was too humiliated by that experience to wanna sharpen it by talking to Kate about it. After all, what good would it do to bring it up now?

"It's okay then," Kate finally said, giving his hand a gentle rub. "I probably would have done the same."

"Done what?"

"Gone out to revenge."

Randy couldn't believe the ease with which couples got into extramarital affairs. Where were the men and women who took vows and lived by them *till death do us part*? Where were the women who would never think of sleeping with a man who wasn't their husband? And where were the husbands who found love only in the arms of a woman they called *my dear wife*?

Randy said, "Kate, didn't your parents teach you that it is wrong to revenge?"

"They did."

"But you'd still revenge anyway?"

"One of those things we do out of anger, you know?"

"I understand. Kind of like what I did, right?"

Kate nodded.

"What I regret, though, is just how acceptable things like anger and revenge seem to have become today. Is it the movies or the glitzy mags?"

"Both, I guess," Kate said even though she wasn't interested in that topic. She took Randy's hand and led him away from the window. Finally standing by the bed, she said, "Honey, do you think we have a chance to start again?"

Randy squeezed her hand. "I know we do."

Kate pulled Randy into the firmness of the new mattress and whispered something in his ear. It was all it took. And good thing was—Bill was not home. Just Randy and Kate and the angels.

Just as God had envisioned it!

———

Bosibori just couldn't shake Vivian off her mind. Who was this woman? Unable to focus on anything at home, she finally decided to call Vivian. She pulled Vivian's number out of her husband's cell phone.

She dialed. "Hello?"

From the other end, it was a soft, sweet voice that answered.

Bosibori said, "Vivian, I am Mrs. Ogwoka."

"Wow, so kind of you to call me, ma'am. You know, I'll be in church tomorrow to hear Pastor Ogwoka's sermon. He has been a great help to me already."

"I'm glad."

But she wasn't glad at all. She was just stuck. She didn't want to confront Vivian now for fear it may turn out the young woman was really out for help and nothing else. What Bosibori didn't know, though, was that the woman who had answered the call was in Mombasa and her name wasn't Vivian.

Her name was Carol, that goddess of sexual perversion.

•

"Who was that?" Jerome asked. He was now relaxed and had already eaten dinner at a restaurant he had never been to before.

Carol turned on the Luciferian Screen and pointed at a sweet, middle-aged woman. "You know her?"

Jerome shook his head.

"That's Pastor Ogwoka's wife."

"Huh? How did she get your number?"

"Jerome, how long will it take you to realize that I can get the phone number of anybody I need to talk to? In this case, though, I had called Pastor Ogwoka earlier in the day; that's how his wife got my number. She thought she was calling Vivian."

"But why would she call Vivian?"

"Just between me and you…she thinks Viv and the pastor have the hots for each other." She winked. "Come. Just look at this."

"What is it?"

Carol pointed at a guy in a shower room and Jerome looked closely at the figure. When the image formed and it turned out to be Pastor Ogwoka, his jaw dropped. "The pastor!"

"It's him."

"Are you saying his wife sneaked and called you thinking you were the pastor's girlfriend?"

"You got it. She thinks the pastor is seeing Vivian."

"But how did that happen?"

Carol kissed him on the cheek. "Let me tell you how I did it…"

SIXTEEN

"**F**irst things first, Jerome!"

Jerome and Carol were in their hotel room in Mombasa. They had been in this coastal city for nearly four hours now. They had already had a sumptuous dinner and even taken a leisurely walk along the palm-lined streets of the slow city. This was a town where folks started their day around ten in the morning. It was at that late hour that laidback folks moved with chameleon speed to secure some form of breakfast, then rolled into businesses and office work; work that gave way to lunch at 12:30. Then at 2:30, folks got back to work and closed for the day at 4:30. This was a world of its own!

But Mombasa *is* a beautiful city. Propped up by tourism, most businesses are designed to cater to the tailored interests of visitors from all over the world who are attracted to the warm, sandy beaches of the Indian Ocean. From busy car rental companies to curio shops to native attire joints, the town is bustling and alive with fun. Besides, there is a strong presence of American military and Italian businesses that create a thriving prostitution ring along the coastal strip. It's because of its primary focus on tourism that commercial activity in the city starts slow and late. *No point opening doors to folks still in bed by nine, right?* That's the attitude of just about everybody.

"First things first? Well, what's on your mind?" Jerome asked, looking Carol in the eye.

Carol scooted and made herself comfortable next to him. It was the fifth floor and the windows here opened up to reveal the tantalizing presence of the early stars and the lackluster glory of the banana moon. From this vantage point, that moon seemed perched right above the waters of the Indian Ocean. Deep in the horizon, there was endless darkness, only broken by the occasional flickers of distant light. The flickers were beams of approaching vessels like ocean liners or cruise ships owned by some of the world's wealthiest merchants or leading Western powers. At least that's what people said.

But Carol knew better. She got behind Jerome and steadied his head. "You see those flickers?"

"Yeah."

"What do you think they are?"

Jerome's eyes narrowed. "Stars in the sea?"

Carol frowned. "What? What does stars in the sea mean?"

"I mean—a reflection of starts?"

Carol smiled. "If that were the case, wouldn't there be a lot more flickers considering the number of stars the heavens have to showcase on any given night?"

"Then what are they?"

"Each flicker is a sub."

"A sub?"

"A submarine, Jerome. Why do you allow yourself to sound so ignorant?"

Jerome didn't mind the put-down. This was too fascinating to be distracted by Carol's harmless put-down. Looking even more intently now, he said, "Carol, why would a submarine be there?"

Carol cleared her throat. There was something *sexy* about the subs to her. They were the epitome of mystery and power. To her, the submarine was like Luciferianism—you knew it was there, but could never understand the way it operated...or even what its mission was.

"Heard my question, Carol? Why is it there?"

Carol said, "The Americans are everywhere. That superpower is the only nation on earth with a capacity to send subs and other prowlers around the waters of the world and still have enough money to feed its people. Those subs shoot to the surface of the seas only occasionally and mostly at night to avoid detection."

"Strange. Does our government know they are there?"

"Sure."

"Doesn't that bother our security folks?"

"Nope. America is an ally."

A moment of awkwardness crept in. Carol knew it was time to start the initiation process, but she was worried that Jerome still appeared tense. This was the only thing she hated—that in spite of the enormous powers the Luciferians had over humans, and their zero-sum dominion of this earth, God had denied them the power to know what was in a *mind*. They could reliably predict what an individual was going to do and even orchestrate things to go a certain way, but they couldn't tell what was in a mind. A man's mind was still a mystery to them. She hated that.

"Jerome?"

"Yes—? It's almost time, right?"

"Not quite."

"But it's close to 11:00 p.m."

"The meeting starts at 2:00 a.m."

Jerome's jaw dropped. "Two? Are you saying we'll have to stay awake till then?"

"You'll be surprised how swiftly time rolls by. In any case, there are certain things we must do before we go to the meeting."

Jerome felt—in his heart—that the time had come. This was his final chance to say no to evil and risk losing his life or sail along with the crested wave of Carol's plans and get rich instantly. His fear, even now, though, was what it would take. Could he risk asking Carol that?

Carol said, "Jerome, you and I have been friends for almost two years even though we've kept our private matters to ourselves. From tonight that will change."

"How?"

"What I've never told you is that in the two years I've known you, the revered Council of Luciferian Knights allowed me to study your temperament and make a judgment on your suitability to go straight from initiation to knighthood. We want you to become a knight!"

"Me? Why? Aren't there agents who can…?"

"No. Well, let me explain. There are agents, but we never really pick knights from within the ranks of agents; knights are picked from folks a knight like me has befriended and found suitable for the role. Trust me, if I had any doubt about your suitability I would never have befriended you." She looked him in the eye and he saw the sparkle that made her look so much like an angel…the mysterious sense of urgency that always made Jerome wonder about her. Feeling she had him, she whispered the verdict in his ear. "Jerome, you are our man!"

"Aren't you bothered that I am a Christian?"

"No. Four of our knights are leading Christians."

"Four? My God! And the rest?"

"One is a Moslem, an influential Middle-Eastern *sheikh* in fact; one is a Jew and the other a Hindu. We don't discriminate. Our focus is to build a global movement that will someday replace the kingdom most Christians believe is coming."

"You mean the much heralded *second coming kingdom*?" Jerome asked, recalling that that's what his pastor always called the awaited return of Christ to this earth to take believers to heaven.

"Yes."

"Carol?" There was a slight tremor in his voice. This was as poignant a moment as he could ever remember in his life. His dalliances with Luciferianism came down to this moment. This was the hour. "I was told that when Christ returns a second time He will take His children to heaven and leave Lucifer in this world for a thousand years without anyone to tempt; that Lucifer and his angels will roam the face of this earth without success. Ever heard of that?"

"Sure."

"What do you make of it?"

"It's crap. The Bible was written by folks who were delusional; others were possibly even deranged. When they wrote that book, most assumed events would unfold exactly as they had predicted, but they were wrong. We have managed to turn the prophecies and predictions of that book into disasters on a magnitude that has made God lose face. In fact, where we haven't orchestrated the chaos ourselves, the predictions of that lame book have come a cropper by themselves. Because of our relentlessness, to folks in Europe, America and Australia, that book is as good as dead. It's only here in Africa that people still linger between two opinions. That will end soon!"

"Fine. Now…if I became a knight, what would that mean for my dear Vivian?"

Carol kept quiet.

"And how will it impact my parents?"

"Like I told you earlier, Jerome, there are certain things I'll only discuss after we've been through the initiation."

"Fine. How about me? What will the impact be?"

Carol cleared her throat. "If wealth is what you want, you'll have it all. We will make you the wealthiest man in Kenya."

"Wealthier than Njonjo?"

"Forget Njonjo."

"Kibs?"

"What does Kibs have?"

"Chandaria?"

"Now we are talking."

"Then listen. I'm in. So can you walk me through what it will take for me to become a knight?"

"The first step is simple enough."

"Which is?"

"Acceptance. You've already done that. I want you to know that from now on you can't back out without inviting grave consequences on yourself." She smiled. "I only say this as a friend, Jerome. Hope you understand?"

"It's okay."

"The next step is also simple."

"Tell me about it."

"By sleeping with me, I instantly transfer my powers to you. It is an act that gives you the ability to see this world and all the events in it through the penetrating, perceptive eyes of a Luciferian. You'll be instantly recognizable to agents and knights around the world and will command instant respect wherever you go...whether in a church, at work or any government office. Get it?"

He nodded.

Then Carol moved to make things happen. She recalled her own initiation, when her own father had ushered her into the brotherhood of Luciferian knights at a ceremony near the Kenya-Tanzania border. Now it was her turn to bring Jerome along.

"But why sex?" Jerome asked.

"Tradition. It's how I pass the *sin* gene to you!"

They got on with it and it was done without passion at all. It was strictly business. When they were done, it was as if Jerome was given a new set of eyes. He felt like a guy who once was blind but now could see. Everywhere he looked, he saw Luciferian agents in action. From one end of the world to another, from culture to culture and from tongue to tongue, the forceful agents were busy wrecking havoc on the world. If it wasn't mass annihilation caused by typhoons in the Philippines, it was a landslide in China, and if it wasn't a landslide, it was a devastating plane crash, and if it wasn't any of those, it was a sudden political upheaval that claimed thousands of lives in Africa or Burma.

"So," Jerome said, taken aback. "Is this the world in color?"

Carol smiled. "It is. You've just acquired the power to see what goes on around the world in real time. You are now a creature above humans and the lower cadre of Luciferian agents. What the angels of God can see you can see too. You are now an angel for our side. The only thing that remains of my tasks is to ask which of your relatives you want to sacrifice to the Holy One."

Strangely, this time Jerome didn't flinch at that question. It was as if the new powers he'd just acquired shielded him from the shock of Carol's words. *Death, blood, sacrifice* and other fear-invoking words were the new normal. Looking her in the eye, he said, "The blood of my father will do."

Carol put her right hand on his head and made the Luciferian pronouncement. "And may the blood of your father—the man who gave you life—bind you forever to the cause of the Holy One." That's all it took. At his home in the village, Jerome's father died quietly in his sleep. And even when Jerome saw his mom, through the aid of the Luciferian Screen, weeping in deep anguish, he didn't feel her pain at all; this was just business, nothing personal.

"And now for the big deal," Jerome said.

"Sure. We leave in a minute."

"Which hotel?"

"It's not a hotel we're going to, Jerome. Let me press this button on the Luciferian Screen so you can see the celestial city where our strategic quinquennial meetings are held." Carol pressed the button and a magnificent city spread across the screen. "Ever been to that city?" she asked as the image magnified and clarified.

Jerome looked closely at the buildings, the layout, the screaming opulence and determined that no, he had never been to any city that dazzling. Could it be Monaco? St. Tropez? Or was it Cancun?

Carol said, "That city is known only to a select few. The agents know where it is…and of course the knights do too."

"Is it in Kenya?"

"Nope."

"Uganda?"

"No."

"Tanzania?"

"Nooo!"

Jerome frowned. "Are you telling me we are about to go to a city abroad and we are still here?"

"Take a look at this," Carol said and pressed a second button. What Jerome saw was a mass of water on the screen and zig zagging pathways that ran down toward the city. Along the pathways there was no activity at all. Just paths!

"A city under water?"

"Isn't it fantastic?"

"It is. But, Carol, are you telling me the Luciferians inherited a city that submerged somewhere?"

"Nope."

"I give up!"

"What I'm telling you is that for the first time in your life you've seen the glorious city of knights. This city is one of the tightest held secrets around the world; not even the prowling U.S. submarines have been able to find it."

"Huh? Are they trying to find it?"

"Officially, no; but secretly we know they are. The CIA and the NIS have never stopped trying to get to the city of knights. We won't let them. We saw the havoc American agents wrecked on the Vatican when they infiltrated the security apparatus in Rome. And by the way, you can see today the sway they hold over the Israelis because, again, they've infiltrated the Mossad. It is never wise to let the curious Americans in on anything. They are never up to any good."

"But don't we have American agents or knights in the city?"

"No. We have folks who were once Americans but are now not. They are now citizens of the city of knights."

"I don't get it."

"It's simple. Once you are officially knighted tonight, you will cease to be a Kenyan. Sure, you'll live in Nairobi, but your passport will have a little watermark that will make it have the weight of a diplomatic passport. Actually, it will have the force of timelessness!"

"Wow. Will I also have other identifying documents that make me a citizen of the city of knights?"

"Yes."

"Like a Luciferian ID?"

"No. It's more like a light that shines on your chest. It is as powerful as it is mysterious. I can't tell you how it works just now, but I can tell you that wherever you go in this world, nobody will stop you at Customs or any other office; and if they do all you have to do is *touch* that light. Its reflective power will flash **Diplomat** in the eyes of the official you're dealing with and they'll let you have access to whatever person or building you need. Tonight we'll use yours."

"My light?"

"Yes."

Jerome looked at his chest and saw that indeed there was a light.

Carol said, "Press it!"

Jerome brought his finger toward the glow as if fearing he might get burned. But again, now that he was about to get knighted, what was there to fear really? He touched his finger to the light and within seconds found himself right before the being John the Revelator described in Revelation as the dragon, the ancient serpent and the fallen angel. This was the being Christians called Satan. So this *is* where he lived?

Carol bowed before the being and asked Jerome to do the same. Within seconds, the vast city lit up with trumpets and lights and agents gathered from around the globe in a matter of seconds. It was amazing to see the city virtually empty one minute, bustling with celestial life the next minute. How glorious was this!

But that was just the beginning. Jerome had just come to the city of knights at the exact same time Carol had said the meeting would start. In just an hour or so, he was going to become the world's newest knight.

His life was about to irreversibly change.

———

In the quiet village where Jerome was born, word of Mzee Ratego's sudden death spread like gushing waters that had burst the banks of River Nyando. People gathered quickly upon the *nduru* of Jerome's mom. When villagers found out what had happened, they were saddened because the old man was loved and respected in the village. Strangely, though, when Jerome's number was dialed, it went unanswered. And when Vivian's was buzzed, she answered but sounded so confused. It was the price that had to be paid for Jerome to become wealthy.

Yes, death too was a tool in the hands of satanic agents.

SEVENTEEN

Pastor Ogwoka had not slept by the time he saw the dull beam of the sun's attempt to smile on Nairobi—yonder. Through the night he had tossed and turned and denied his insomniac ways whenever his equally troubled wife confronted him to say what was bothering him. Content to say only that Bosibori already knew what was eating him up slowly, he was determined to deal with this matter as a man; he wasn't going to let Bosibori be party to his travails in case the Luciferians decided to come after his life. This was his cross to carry, not his family's.

But now the sun was rising and soon he would have to be in church. Through the week things had gone well; nothing out of the ordinary had transpired between Monday and Thursday. Then came Friday. That was the day the aggressive Luciferians had decided to invade his space. Without warning, they suddenly took over his agenda and altered completely his frame of mind. No, he could no longer preach about the second coming and tithing, he now had a more pressing matter to handle. He had to deal with the Luciferians.

"Good morning, my dear husband?"

Pastor Ogwoka knew his wife well. Whenever things were okay she always greeted him with a smile and said *How are you, sweetheart?* Noting the departure from the norm on her part, he guarded himself just like he had all night. He said, "I just thought of something!"

"Something so important that you won't greet me this morning?" She turned to face him. "How was your night?"

"Frankly, not good."

"It's that girl, right?"

The pastor drew a deep breath and started to lift himself off the bed. He slapped away the comforter and came up on his elbow. Casting a sideway glance at his unimpressed wife, he said, "I've got to prepare. Have to work on my sermon."

"Your sermon? As far as I recall you prepared that sermon on Tuesday and called it done. Did you think of something to add to it?"

"No. I'm not preaching it."

Bosibori got up too. "Why not?"

"You know why already."

'It's the girl, right?"

Pissed but keeping his anger in check, the weary pastor said, "Sweetheart, why are you focused on that girl? Are you unable to see the bigger picture? We are dealing here with a force that could destroy our church. These people are not your average human beings."

"I know," Bosibori said, cutting him off. "That's why the girl worries me. How sure are you she's not one of them?"

"I'm not sure."

"If she is, don't you see that you've suddenly brought yourself to a point where you're talking to the devil? Can't you see that she might well be the woman they've chosen to bring you down?"

"You may be right."

"I know I am."

Pastor Ogwoka got off the bed and went to the bathroom to shower. He always did his best thinking in there, so when Bosibori asked to tag along and shower with him, he found a way to wiggle out of it. He wanted to be alone. To reflect. To play back what he'd been through since yesterday. It was while in there that he decided he wouldn't write another sermon. The one he had would do just fine.

After showering, he walked out and dressed quickly. Being a rather somber day, he wore his dark suit, a white shirt and a maroon tie. Finally set, he told Bosibori not to worry about breakfast. "I'll eat later, when the service is over."

"You'll preach in an empty stomach?"

"I will."

"Why?"

"I need to be in the office. I want to meditate, to plead with the Lord to bless my ministry."

Bosibori walked up to him and looked him in the eye. "Tell me something—are you scared?"

He looked down. He didn't want to admit it, but he was really scared. How could he not be? He was just flesh and blood and it seemed he was suddenly in the middle of a harrowing, decisive battle between good and evil.

"Are you?"

"Sweetheart, I would be lying if I said I'm not, but I want you to realize one thing—that the God we serve is greater than any evil the devil may shoot our way. We will win this war!"

"Then go out there and lead the forces of good!"

"Huh?" Pastor Ogwoka was stunned by his wife's sudden macho attitude. "You want me to go fight?"

"Don't let evil win!"

"Thank you, sweetheart. Then I'll see you later."

Pastor Ogwoka left the house and drove straight to the church. As he did, he kept wondering what had become of Jerome. Had the guy gone forward with his plan to meet the

Luciferians? Had he joined the movement? And where was he now?

His phone rang.

"Hello?"

It was Jerome. From Mombasa, Jerome said, "Pastor Ogwoka, I'll be in Nairobi later this evening. Can we meet?"

The pastor's breath caught. Why did Jerome want a meeting? Had he succeeded in keeping the Luciferians at bay? Did he now want to spill the beans about the MO of that dreadful group of people? Or was this call part of that elaborate plan to infiltrate and destroy the church of God through him?

"Can we make it six?" Jerome asked.

Pastor Ogwoka agreed.

"Then let's talk later." *Click.*

On that note, Pastor Ogwoka drove on to church and locked himself up in the office. He wanted to talk to God quietly; ask God why He had allowed the Luciferians to invade the church. But just as he knelt beside his desk and started to pray, the phone rang again.

"Hello?"

"Pastor, it's Vivian."

"Morning, Vivian. I had just started praying."

"At home?"

"No. I'm in the office already."

"That's good. Pray for me."

"Will do."

"And remember, I'll see you at church later."

"Okay. God bless."

But Vivian wasn't gonna see him at church later; she was on her way already. Guessing rightly that a pastor dealing with some of the most decisive issues of his career wouldn't want to be home too long on a Saturday morning, Vivian had woken up by 5:30, showered and had breakfast. She had gone on to dress up elegantly, being careful to avoid excessive adornment. Finally ready, she had decided to call and find out if the pastor may have gone to the office early, as she had suspected he would. And indeed he had. He was in.

She drove straight to the church and managed to get there before any of the deacons or deaconesses arrived. It was gonna be just her and the pastor. And her plan was simple—to get the pastor to declare his erotic interest in her; the rest would follow later. If he wanted everything now, however, she was dressed in a skimpy enough manner that giving herself to him wouldn't be a problem.

It didn't take long for her to get to the church. Out of the blue, Pastor Ogwoka heard a soft knock on the door and wondered which of the dutiful church officers may have made it to the sanctuary so early. He got up and opened the door.

"Vivian!"

"Sorry if I interrupted anything, Pastor."

"No, you didn't. I was just praying. Please, come in."

"Thanks."

"Have a seat."

Vivian took a seat and looked down to avoid going eye to eye with the pastor. She didn't want to appear disrespectful—and didn't want her intentions easily read.

"So, Vivian," Pastor Ogwoka started calmly. "What brings you to church this early?"

Vivian's head stayed down. She didn't answer right away. Her plan was to be discrete, make her intentions obvious without scaring off the minister or seeming like this was something she did on a regular basis. Looking cheap wasn't anything she desired.

"Have you heard from Jerome?" the pastor asked.

"No."

"I did."

Vivian was startled. "What did he say?"

"He'll be in town later this evening."

"And…?"

"He wants to meet me."

"Strange. Does that mean he didn't go through with it?"

Pastor Ogwoka hesitated. He didn't know whether Jerome had gone through with it or not. What he knew for sure was that if Jerome had done it, he was coming back to Nairobi an extremely dangerous man. So, was it really wise to meet a man like that?

"Did he, Pastor?"

"To be honest, I have not the slightest idea."

This is such a dead topic, Vivian thought. In that moment, she decided to switch. "Tell me," she said. "What are you going to preach about?"

Pastor Ogwoka tensed. The hair on his back stood. Why was this girl really here? And why did she look a lot more radiant than when they first met? Could Bosibori have been right about Vivian being a closet Luciferian?

"Pastor, are you going to take on devil worshippers?"

He finally found her eyes and held. "Should I?"

"Seems to me like you have no choice."

"Meaning?"

"Meaning your church is in grave danger if you don't take a firm stand and warn about the danger of consorting with the agents of the underworld. The stakes are too high!"

Pastor Ogwoka thought long and hard, then he said, his eyes penetrating Vivian's, "Are you one of them?"

The question caught Vivian completely off-guard. How could Pastor Ogwoka think she was a devil worshipper? Did she look or act like one? Did she even talk like one?

"Are you, Vivian?"

"Of course not!"

"Then why do you look so radiant today?"

"I do?"

"There's something mysterious about you today."

"No," she shot back. "It's not mystery, it's charm."

"Charm?"

"Seductive charm, Pastor. I'm here because I'm attracted to you. Haven't you noticed?"

Alarm bells rang, but was this the time to flee or what? Was this the time to ask Vivian to ship out or keep her just a little while longer? If he had held out for evidence of Vivian's duplicity, wasn't this it?

"Look, Vivian," he said. "I am a minister of the gospel. The Lord has called me, and members of my church have ordained me, to call people to Christ. You are a beautiful woman; a married woman; and you have a wonderful husba…"

"He's a money-chasing scoundrel," she blurted.

"Vivian, respect this office!"

"Jerome is a womanizer!"

Pastor Ogwoka now got up. This was getting out of hand fast. Besides, he feared that the deacons were about to start arriving and a picture of him with Vivian would look suspect and present fodder for tongues that were ever ready to wag. Having been a pastor for a long time, he knew just how easy it was for a scandal to erupt out of nothing. He had seen it many times.

"Pastor, I'm ready for you even now!"

"Get out, Vivian. Out of my office—now!!!"

"If you touch me I'll scream."

Pastor Ogwoka thought about her threat and lowered his tone. He had to try a different approach. He pleaded with Vivian to leave, even attempted to gently lead her out, but she'd have none of it. She wanted the pastor to make love to her in the church office! Instead of leaving, she pasted herself on the frightened minister, her V-neck top parting so he could see the tantalizing curvature of her jutting breasts. Fearing that whoever walked through that door right now wouldn't understand what this was about, he pulled back from her and tried to shove her out.

Right then, Agnes, the deaconess in charge of coordinating the collection of tithes and offering this Sabbath, knocked and pushed back the door as she usually did. In that moment, she saw the pastor's hand on Vivian's breast region, where he was frantically trying to cover them up. Stunned by what was going on, Agnes shut the door quietly and left. It was just too much!

Horrified, the pastor, his eyes forming tears, looked Vivian in the eye and said, "You have just destroyed my ministry!"

"I've done nothing wrong," she said innocently.

"So now that you've accomplished your mission, why don't you just leave?"

"I'm going nowhere."

"Then I have to call security."

But he didn't have a chance to. Because just as he was about to dial, Jerome knocked—and just like the deaconess—he pushed back the door and let himself in.

The pastor's hour of reckoning had come.

———

Kate woke up and was about to go to the bathroom to shower when her phone rang. It was Viv calling. "Guess what just happened," she said as soon as Kate answered.

"What now?"

"I may have brought down Pastor Ogwoka."

"Huh? Why? How?"

"A churchwoman found him in my arms!"

"This early?"

"Come to the Remnant Church, okay?"

Because of the way Vivian said it, the urgency in her voice, the mischief of it, Kate woke up Randy and Bill and asked them to prepare quickly. "We are going to the Remnant Church!"

"But why? I wanna go to Ebenezer," Randy shot back. "What I need today is Pastor Matemu's intellectual sermons."

"Randy, news is breaking fast and furious at the Remnant Church. Pastor Ogwoka has been caught!"

"Caught doing what?"

"Bad things."

Instantly, Randy knew that things were going to get downright ugly. The pastor had somehow allowed himself to get entangled with the Luciferians. But how could the Holy Spirit have failed to open his eyes so he could see the devil worshippers for who they really were?

His tear dropped!

EIGHTEEN

Carol was elated by the scripted way things had turned out in Mombasa. Her plan had worked to the script. Now she was back in her sprawling, leafy home to scheme her final act. According to the Luciferian game plan, she was supposed to be the last of the feared Indian Ocean knights. The secret Indian Ocean city was to be moved to the Pacific, where the future of Luciferianism was steadily focused. If things played to the letter, Carol was slated to become second in command to the holy, the most high, that ancient angel of light. Lucifer himself!

But there was just one final agenda item on her desk. She was tasked by the Luciferians to activate a seed that was planted in a young girl called Kate nearly thirty years ago. It was at a school Kate attended. On the night the seed was planted, Kate had been asleep on her bed in a dormitory she shared with the town-dwelling form twos. At around 2:00 a.m., one of the Luciferians in the dorm made her way to Kate's bed and stood next to her with an assortment of paraphernalia she kept a top secret in the dorm. What followed was a swift operation that lasted just under five seconds. In that time, the agent cut a tiny incision on Kate's neck and shoved a tiny speck into it. Kate didn't feel a thing!

Today, because of the ongoing restructuring at the top echelons of Luciferianism, all the work in Africa had to be scaled down. This was in an effort to direct the nucleus of each operation to the Pacific. Kate, being one of the two women in Kenya who still carried one of those Luciferian specks, had to be tracked down and activated. The time for her to take her rightful place in the movement had come. Carol had to act now to bring her in.

Because it was a Saturday morning, the day after the deeply inspiring meeting in the city under the vast waters of the Indian Ocean, Carol was in excellent spirits. She felt it in her bone that the Luciferians were on the verge of decapitating *Remnantism*, paralyzing Catholicism and disorienting the wider Protestant establishment in Kenya. The mission for which Carol was born was about to be achieved. Then she'd be transformed into eternal glory—first as Lucifer's number two, then as an equal of that ancient angel. The belief was that in the days before Luciferian conquest of the world, that angel would need a female by his side...then the two would jointly rule the new world.

But aware that winning Kate's trust was not going to be like cutting ghee with a red-hot blade, she decided to turn on her screen and watch the woman's movements. She wanted to be familiar with Kate's ways, feel the beat of her rhythm. It was while the penetrating power of that screen was focused on the home Randy and Kate lived in that Carol saw the Sabbath morning preparations going on there. Randy was dressed, Bill was dressed and so was Kate. It was obvious it was a Sabbath Day and the family was about to leave for church. The only thing Carol needed to know now was which one.

It didn't take long before the cunning Carol had her answer. Like Vivian, Randy and Kate were going to the Remnant Church, that huge church along Milimani Road where a pastor was caught with a woman this morning. Delighted that Kate had chosen that church, Carol dressed up and got herself ready for worship too. It was time to execute her final mission on earth, because after this—she would never be human again. She was set to join the handful of human agents who had gone all the way to become celestials.

Time ticked by fast. The clouds that had gathered earlier across the Nairobi skyline had now cleared, giving way to sharp rays that seemed to pierce the clouds with the force of a fired projectile. In spite of the rays, though, a sense of gloom still pervaded the church perimeter. It was as if people could tell something crazy was in the offing. But it wasn't until 10:30 that Randy and Kate finally walked into the church itself in spite of the fact that they had come through the gate nearly half an hour earlier. They had deliberately lingered in the lawns around the church to sniff rumor and innuendo from those who had come in earlier. They wanted to know what folk thought.

This large church, originally built on a plot that was designed to stand a house of worship away from the city centre, was now swallowed up and stood at a place where the city and its corrupting influences was felt like a pimple on a supermodel's face. Built in the nineties through the sacrificial donations of dedicated members, the three thousand-capacity sanctuary was one of the largest churches in Africa. Its less-than-flashy pews were arranged in a manner that created five rows. Those rows opened up into long walkways that stretched from the two main doors at the back right to the deep front.

As Kate led the way to the front, Bill and Randy followed. The two men in her life hated to sit at the front, but there was nothing they could do once Kate's mind was made up. They watched with displeasure as the lady made her way deep to the front and drop into the middle pew, where the only form of obstruction between her and the minister was the empty space between her and the pulpit.

As Randy sank into the pew and scooted next to Kate, he made a face and whispered, "What in the world is this about?"

"Worship," Kate said.

"Worship indeed. Then what's this chic doing here?"

Kate smiled. "What's wrong with her being here, Bill? Are you saying my secretary can't come to church with me?"

"I smell a rat."

"Suit yourself," Kate said. She put her hand out and Vivian took it in an exaggerated handshake. Randy watched the two women out the corner of his eye and concluded that something strange was going on here. Either Kate and Vivian were still in love and wanted to paint it on his face or he was here to witness the beginning of a firestorm. Whatever it was, his instincts warned him to gear up for a major shake. This was going to be exciting.

And indeed, he didn't have to wait long. Barely thirty minutes into his reluctant arrival here, Randy heard whispers and observed extraordinary excitement in faces that normally maintained a studious cool. Right behind him, two elderly women were embroiled in a charged argument about Pastor Ogwoka. "How long will you defend that sleazy character? He was caught with a woman in his office just this morning, okay?" one said, doing little to hide her disdain for the minister.

"*Uongo*—lies!" the other shot back with venom.

"It's true. A deaconess caught the man red-handed. His roving hand was on the young woman's breast. On it!"

"Really? Do we know the woman?"

"Nope. We don't know her."

Randy shook his head in disbelief. Unable to contain himself, he tapped Kate on the shoulder and said, "Can you believe these two women behind us?"

"What's up with them?"

"Just listen."

Kate leaned back like a shy thief. She did it just in time to catch the women predict that if what was being rumored about the pastor was true, he would be dismissed from the ministry or transferred to another church. "The Remnant Church has very high standards when it comes to matters of morality and professional ethics," the more sympathetic woman said. "I pray this is made-up stuff."

Vivian looked at the two women and made a face. Then turning to Kate, she whispered. Her words were calculated to make Kate know that she was a key player in the unfolding drama. She said, "Kate, there's no way I'll let Pastor Ogwoka be dismissed. He did nothing wrong!"

Kate turned and her eyes narrowed. "He did nothing wrong? How can you say that with such confidence?"

"So you didn't believe me? I was the woman, Kate!"

Kate's jaw dropped. So Vivian was serious? Staring in disbelief, she leaned in and said, "I can't believe you had the audacity to trap this innocent pastor. But that is not important now. It has happened. What you must do, and do it urgently, is speak up. You must let folk in this church know that Pastor Ogwoka is innocent."

"But how will I do that?"

As they talked, a young lady glided to the pulpit and urged those within her hearing to turn to their hymnals. "It's time to praise the Lord in songs," she said very sweetly. And with that song service started. Enthusiastic worshipers sang for the next twenty minutes…going from *Onward Christian Soldiers* to *I Must Tell Jesus*. For Vivian—who had been a regular at the supercharged Pentecostal services—this was rather lackadaisical and lacked the fire that set ablaze the atmosphere in the more upbeat Sunday services. Regardless, she found something deeply inspiring about these songs in the Remnant hymnal. Their words were organized into thoughts that made sense and told a coherent story. They had the impact of telling the story of Christ in a profoundly new way; something she had never heard anywhere.

Because of the depth of the words, Vivian was stunned to see that most of the folks in this church—though clearly enthusiastic in that conservative mode they were accustomed to in this upscale sanctuary—were devoid of the zeal that translated the words of the songs into something that made the Jesus story become a force that transformed lives. It was as if at a certain level worship had become routine, something parents did for the sake of their children and to socialize; and children did because Daddy and Mommy wanted them to.

Right in the middle of that song service, the pulpit party walked in from the vestry to take seats behind the glassy, flower-decked pulpit. Like was the emerging trend in churches across the world, the party consisted of a child, who would tell the children's story, a woman, for the sake of gender-sensitivity, one of the many elders, who made the announcements, and the pastor, usually the one slated to speak.

Unlike other Sabbaths, though, Pastor Ogwoka looked somber. His face, even though he tried hard to project effusiveness and a sense of calm, bore the marks of pain and rare discouragement. Only minutes ago, his Head Elder and other church officials had tried to stop him from preaching, but he had dismissed their fears. "I'm innocent," he had asserted with the conviction of a man led by the Holy Spirit. "Listen, the deaconess didn't see me do anything wrong, she saw what she thought looked wrong, that's all."

"But word has spread like bushfire, Pastor Ogwoka," the Head Elder had pleaded. "Can't we wait till this storm is over before you can speak to the church again?"

Pastor Ogwoka would have none of it. There was a lot more at stake than just rumor about being caught with a woman. If he missed this one chance to strike a blow at the heart of the Satanists, the problem would explode within days and morph into a hydra-like monster that would be impossible to contain. But that wasn't even his biggest worry. The larger issue here was the credibility of the church. He didn't want the church's enhanced image trashed by the acts of a reckless young woman and the tactlessness of a motherly deaconess who should have known better than talk carelessly.

For those who had already heard the rumor, though, watching Pastor Ogwoka behind that pulpit was too painful an episode. They knew their pastor well. He was a good man. A family man. A man of God. How could the devil have cornered such a dedicated saint?

Then it was time for tithe and offerings, which was done in a matter of minutes to give way to a special item of music. That item was offered by the resurgent church choir, directed by the energetic director just acquired from Tanzania. As the choir sang, the pastor sat pensively. He wondered why church members—over the years—had always been quick to believe accusations leveled against ministers. And why it was that these days when a pastor wanted to scheme the downfall of another he felt free to divulge info to the press; info that trashed the name of a fellow pastor and ruined the credibility of the church. What had happened to the good old days when Christians saw themselves as members of a closely-knit family where problems, however intricate, were solved within the confines of grace and loving tears? Where was the loving church of Pastor Isaac Okeyo and Pastor Mwamakamba? Where was the unified movement Elder Bazzara and Pastor Neal C. Wilson worked so hard to pass on to posterity?

"Pastor?"

Pastor Ogwoka leaned over. It was the child preacher. She said, "I feel so scared, Pastor."

Pastor Ogwoka managed a gentle smile at first, then leaning deeper, he said, "Natalie, don't be scared. When you get up there, just tell your story then walk right back here like a princess and take your seat next to me. Can you do that for me?"

Natalie thought for a sec, then she nodded, but added, "Well, I have an idea, Pastor."

"What is it?"

"Maybe you can stand next to me?"

Without blinking, Pastor Ogwoka agreed. Minutes later, when Natalie's time to narrate her story came, the minister stood next to her. The story she beautifully narrated was about a shy little girl who was punished by her teacher because of the false witness of another girl who thought she saw what she claimed she saw. It was only after the girl had been punished that the real offender stepped forward. When the girl who had been punished was asked what she wished to see done to the classmate who had witnessed against her, she said, "Forgive her. She didn't mean to lie!"

"Are you sure?" the teacher had asked.

"That's what Jesus would do, right?"

Pastor Ogwoka's tears formed. He couldn't help but wonder whether someone had told little Natalie to tell this very story. But such considerations had to wait because as soon as the choir sang, the next voice the congregation was to hear was his.

Sitting there like it was his first time ever in this church, he prayed that the Lord would give him the words to use on a day like this.

And the Lord did. When the minister got up to speak, it became evident from the get go that this was going to be a sermon like no other preached before in this church. He started it by making the provocative statement that the tireless Luciferians have invaded our church. After the explosive statement, he went on to narrate—in painful detail—how the week had played out. He talked about his encounter with Jerome, then Vivian, then Carol. He didn't mention them by name, but Randy knew who he was talking about. Finally he talked about Jerome's dramatic visit to Mombasa and his arrival in Nairobi just this morning. "As soon as he arrived, he came straight to my office. He looked mysterious and was clearly a man on an end-time mission. Our church is under siege!" he thundered.

"It is true," Vivian said. She shot off her seat and made her way toward the pulpit. Some scandalized elders and deacons dashed forward to try to restrain her, but Pastor Ogwoka asked them to let her come. She walked up with urgency—as if she was possessed of something—and asked the calm pastor to let her talk.

"You may," the pastor said.

"I'm not one of you," she started. "But I have friends who are. Today those friends didn't invite me here. I invited them. If you wonder who I am, I am Vivian—the woman Pastor just talked about. It is true that I came to his office to seek help with my husband who I have since learned has become a leading Luciferian after undergoing initiation last night in Mombasa. I have lost the fight to keep my husband from ruin. I stand here now because I don't want to see another man go down through no fault of his own

"As I sat there and listened to Natalie's story, I made up my mind that I would get up and talk if a chance presented itself. I apologize that I have seen this hour as my chance, against the wishes of the elders. What I want to say is that Pastor Ogwoka is an honorable, decent man. It was I who brought myself to him. When the deaconess he just talked about walked in and saw his hand on me, it was because he was pushing me out of his office after I had made him aware of my intentions.

"But people of God, I am not a Luciferian as Pastor Ogwoka has declared. I am just a young woman who wanted to date the most dashing pastor I have ever met. That has failed. So let me say what I know for sure. Truth is—the Luciferians are here. I don't mean to cause panic in this church, but Luciferianism, just like Christianity, is not a thing to wear on a sleeve; it is in the heart. In a congregation this size, Lucifer, that cunning angel of light, has planted a lot of followers. His followers are the ones you will see campaign for positions. They are the ones you will see huddled in corners of three to gossip and scheme against fellow church members. They are the ones you will see broadcasting their wealth by showing off their tinted-window fuel-guzzlers and supper expensive garments. They do such things because their master has planted in them the same heart he had before he was kicked out of heaven. A heart of unmitigated pride.

"I stand before you this morning to warn that the Luciferians know their time is short. They see the Church—this Church—as the biggest threat to their conquest of the world. My word to you is—the time to turn your hearts fully to Christ is now. Christ knows His people by what is in their hearts just like

Lucifer knows his by what he sees in their hearts. I dare say nothing more."

She sat without another word.

In Muthaiga, Jerome and Carol watched with growing alarm as Vivian warned the very church the Luciferians had targeted for decisive destruction. Shaking her head indignantly, Carol said, "Her time has come, Jerome!"

Jerome agreed. "So her blood must flow now, you mean?"

"Do it!"

From Muthaiga, Jerome took a pointed sword painted with the blood of saints killed across the globe and drove it through Vivian's neck. He then watched with glee as she went down and her blood was received in the underworld.

At the Remnant Church, though, it was a whole different story. Vivian's sudden death was attributed to her carelessness in touching a man of God with sin-stained hands.

She had brought death on herself, they said.

———

Kate couldn't believe Vivian was dead. Even as she stood in the Lee Funeral Home, watching the lifeless body of her friend, it seemed just like a bad dream. But it was also while she was in there that Jerome and Carol walked in. In one swift move, Carol gave Kate a hug and touched her finger against that little speck planted in Kate's neck nearly three decades ago. It was in that hour, as the speck started to work in her, that Kate for the first time saw Vivian for what she really was. Vivian was a Luciferian tasked to corrupt Christian hearts by peddling sex.

That was the reason she was a lesbian, a straight, a bisexual and an angel at ease with any form of sexual activity.

Unlike Kate, however, Vivian's secret status as a Luciferian had never been revealed to her. Not until today. In her death!

NINETEEN

It felt like a brave new world!

Kate and Randy were just back from viewing Vivian's lifeless body when the full impact of the speck's effects set in. She was in the bedroom. Stunned by the clarity of her mind and the sudden images and sounds she was hearing, she dashed back to the living room, where Randy had his eyes on the screen— CNN's *Inside Africa*. Isha Sesay was on with global updates. Back in London, at this hour, Pope Benedict XVI was just concluding his successful visit to the UK and was being seen off at Birmingham International by Prime Minister Cameron and top-ranking officials of the Catholic Church in England.

Kate stormed into the living room and looked Randy in the eye. She said, "Honey, I see the world better now!"

Randy ignored her.

"Randy, I see the world in a way I've never seen it before."

Randy finally unplugged his eyes off the screen and focused them on Kate. What he saw stunned him. Kate's eyes were as bright as a laser beam. They were bright as if she'd had an encounter with a divine force. But more than that, her whole bearing was one that set her apart from other humans now. She was like an angel!

"Kate!"

"It's a fascinating world indeed," Kate said. "We are at war with the followers of that ancient liar; that God who drove Lucifer from heaven and is now trying to run him out of this world too."

"Kate!"

"It's a world where our determined forces and agents have pulled off spectacular victories, decimated whole populations and are now drawing up the largest war plan ever imagined in the history of the universe. This is big…the Armageddon!"

Randy couldn't believe his ears. What had happened to Kate? How could a pastor's daughter utter such blasphemous words?

"Randy, for the first time I see that there is a small light shining in your heart. That light, for a true Christian, should shine brighter though. The amazing thing is that as I look around the world right now, there are not many Christians with a light brighter than yours. You know what that tells me? It tells me that if Christ were to come back today He would find just a handful of faithfuls to take back to heaven. Lucifer has conquered the world!"

"Shut up, Kate," Randy barked.

Kate made a face, then came to his ear. "Randy, are you afraid of the truth?"

"Blasphemy is what it is!"

"Call it whatever you wish, but as we speak this very hour, our agents are active in Nairobi, throughout Kenya and around the world. We have people working to defeat God. Look at it this way—in the village we have the witch doctor and the night runner and the harlot, in the city we have the flashy, sophisticated Luciferian, and in politics and big business there is the *sangoma*. But that is nothing compared to the most effective agents we have out there. Where is that God you always talk about? If He was so great, how come we've managed to destroy a world He created and are now busy running Him out of the hearts of the people He created? He is fallen...that God. He is finished!"

Randy drew a deep breath and let it out in quick succession. He hated to ask, but just had to. "Did you just say *effective agents*?"

"The *tama* type."

"*Tama?* What do you mean?"

"*Tama n'goch alayo*. This is the pastor whose only agenda in the church is to cause maximum disunity. The sweet thing is that this pastor works for the Luciferian agenda without even being aware of it. Tell you what—we love the *tama* pastor."

"Hold on, Kate. Why do you speak as if you are one of them? Have you suddenly become a Luciferian?"

Kate didn't answer that question right away. Since last night, she had put Randy on a roller coaster ride. She had revealed two devastating secrets and watched as her husband had absorbed the body blows. Aware that a third secret, so close to the first two, would have the impact of shifting tectonic plates, she tried to dodge the question all together. In that very moment, however, the city built under the Indian Ocean opened up and Kate, for the first time, saw the glory and majesty of Lucifer. The Holy One was perched on a golden throne, clad in a white robe. To his left, right and back was an angelic being that sang Holy Holy Holy to him. He looked just like the being the Bible called The Son of God!

"Are you a Luciferian, Kate?"

"I've seen Vivian," Kate said.

"Seen who?" Randy finally heard enough. *She's seen a dead woman?* Either Kate was faking it all—which seemed unlikely given the depth of detail—or she urgently needed psychiatric attention.

"Listen up, Randy. Vivian's work on this side is over. She has been called to work in the celestial city. I can see her now, happy as can be, flying with messages from one end of the world to the other. And guess what? Those messages are from the very top."

"Kate, I'll ask you one more time. Here it is. Are you a Luciferian?"

And finally the stage was set. The truth had to come out tonight. All those years of marital bliss were about to crystallize into this one moment. This one answer.

This was the third secret.

TWENTY

In every church organization there is a unit of the organizational structure that deals with matters of the kind that had occurred at the Remnant Church. Within the rapidly-growing Remnant Church, that unit was called Remnant Church Synod. Nestled deep in the leafy woods of Kiambu, RCS, as proud faithfuls popularly referred to the regional office, ran churches within Nairobi Province, Central Kenya and sections of the Rift Valley Province. It was the body that oversaw strategic planning, pastoral transfers and enforced discipline within the ranks.

Tonight, because of what had happened at the Remnant Church earlier in the day, the available members of the executive committee of RCS were summoned to an impromptu consultative meeting. Fearing that the events at the Remnant Church would find their way to the press and cast the broader Christian denomination in a negative light, the executive director and his supporting officers called the meeting to strategize. The idea was to swiftly deal with the matter and counter any harmful reporting that would inevitably grace the penetrating editorial and society pages of the *Sunday Nation*, *Sunday Standard* and the notoriously forceful reporting of the innuendo-laden *Citizenship*.

For Pastor Ogwoka, however, the impromptu meeting, to which he was invited as a key witness, was an opportunity to clear his name before the deeply scandalized church elders and warn them about the aggressiveness of the Luciferians in targeting his church. He wanted to let the elders know that the only way to defeat the devil's wily schemes was to unite; to proclaim God's grace for fallen man from one end of the synod to another and eventually throughout Kenya.

But when Pastor Ogwoka got to the Synod boardroom and sat behind the hardwood table, the chilly reception that greeted him was a warning that the elders were not in a jolly mood at all. It soon became obvious that the elders hadn't called him to sympathize; he was here to be grilled and disciplined. What he couldn't understand was why the elders had made up their minds without giving him a hearing at all. Couldn't they withhold judgment?

The boardroom was large enough to hold about forty people seated comfortably. It was painted cream, a color that made the walls recede and created the impact of a larger, brighter space than was real. A picture of Christ—a little lamb in His hand, a shepherd's rod in the other— hung on the wall usually reserved for the chief. The other walls boasted picture rolls, a feature of traditional Christianity that was still found in Africa but was long relegated to the realm of archives in most of the West and the Americas.

In the middle of the room stood an expansive table. The table was surrounded by comfortable leather chairs, complete with side and back cushions that usually played the unwanted role of nursing delegates to sleep whenever a matter up for discussion turned dry and dreary. At the four corners there were cactus-decorated flower vases, one of which shot back an imaginative impression of one of the pharaohs of ancient Egypt. The vases were covered at the top with spread-out roses and some of the brightest carnations the office hostess had ever brought to the premises. The floor was tiled and was clean in spite of the sticky, red soil of the region. One fluorescent bulb hung just below the ceiling and retained the luster it had come with into the office.

It was in this office, nestled deep in the sprawling building, that some of the most momentous decisions of the Remnant Church in Central Province had been made over the years. Pastors had been transferred from one church to another in the region by the action of committees that met right here. And decisions about the policy direction of the global church were disseminated to local churches by departmental directors who took marching orders from meetings constituted right here. But tonight things couldn't have been farther from the ordinary. No executive committee or EXCOM had ever had to deal with devil worship. To most pastors here, the devil was an abstract concept; a scary being vividly portrayed in biblical passages but not given real life even therein. The devil, to these men, was an idea to be fought, just like communism or the misguided theology of righteousness by works. Indeed, if the devil walked into this boardroom clad in a pinstriped, blue Italian suit, these leaders would gladly welcome and even entertain his suggestions. If he didn't look dark and ugly and scary and had claws and looked like a giant, then he wasn't the devil.

And that's just what worried Pastor Ogwoka. Events of the past three days had revealed to him just how dangerous it was to make assumptions about the devil. He was real. He was immediate. And he was swift. But more than that, he was *a man* and *a woman* who knew that this earth's history was about to close and needed to take as many souls to eternal damnation as possible. Moving his lips in a soft prayer, Pastor Ogwoka decided that the time to warn the leaders gathered here about the perils the church faced was now. This was his only chance.

The meeting started with a prayer. Then, within minutes of its start, it cruised from slow to top-speed. Pastor Ogwoka was given the floor to describe what had been going on at the Remnant Church over the past week. He did. Then he was asked why he hadn't bothered to alert Synod leaders that he was dealing with something of a magnitude this large. He gave a convincing reason, which was this: "Just like each of you seated here, my elders, when the devil came to me in person he looked just too ordinary to scare me. He didn't look like that fire-spitting dragon portrayed in our picture rolls and in our children's literature."

"What's that supposed to mean?" the executive director asked.

"First he was a car salesman, then he was a very rich woman I've seen in my church many times, and finally he was the cunning woman who confronted me in my church this morning. She was…"

"Hold on, Pastor," the executive secretary cut in. "When you say the woman confronted you, are you saying her visit was unplanned?"

"Of course it was unplanned. I had gone to my office to prepare my sermon when I heard her knock. The rest is now history."

"But you believe she was a Luciferian, right?" the scandalized executive secretary pressed.

"I know she was!"

"What makes you so sure?"

Pastor Ogwoka cleared his throat. He wanted to talk at length, use such simple language that by the time he was done the elders would not only empathize, but would also sense the danger the church was facing. But just as he started to talk a soft tap, like a silent knock, was heard on the door. When the executive secretary pried the door open, since he was the one nearest to it, there was no one. And the thing was—the corridor was too long for anyone to have made their way out within the few seconds he had made it to open. *Very strange*, he thought.

He sat.

A knock again.

The executive secretary frowned. "There was nobody there!" He walked back to the door and opened.

No one!

Troubled, the man went back and dropped into his chair, but this time he felt really uneasy. Something didn't add up here.

Another knock. This time louder.

But this time—even before the executive secretary could get up to answer the door—lights slowly dimmed in the room and blasted total darkness through the entire perimeter. Seconds later, footsteps were heard in the room even though everybody was seated.

From her screen in Muthaiga, Carol and Jerome watched with glee as the pastors trembled. The two were impressed by the way Vivian had flown back into Nairobi and was now terrorizing these men of God.

Pastor Ogwoka, though, aware of what was going on, got up and lifted his eyes up in prayer. He called on the Almighty God to vindicate Himself at such a time as this. *Don't allow Satan to triumph tonight*, he whispered. *Let your majesty shine through right now*. In that very moment, the lights flickered and turned back on and the footsteps died down. When Pastor Ogwoka sat down this time, none of the stunned Synod leaders felt brave enough to continue the grilling. The executive director, blown away by his first direct encounter with the Luciferians, stood up and asked the officers to pray.

But that's not how Pastor Ogwoka wanted things to play out. No. These elders needed to understand what was going on here. He said, "My elders, I am just a humble servant of the Gospel of Christ, but if you'll allow me, I want to suggest that we consecrate ourselves to Christ afresh tonight. I say so because I am aware that the moment we leave this place the Luciferians are going to come after us with the zeal of a hungry cat after a well-fed rat. They will try to kill us. Torture us. Attack our friends and families. They'll do whatever it takes to derail our mission of advancing the cause of Christ." He drew a deep breath, then releasing it in squirts of pain, said, "My elders, the approach tonight is not prayer, but total consecration. The final battle between God and Satan has started tonight. This is the end of time!"

"Pastor Ogwoka is absolutely right," the executive director said. And looking at the pastor, the executive director saw a new radiance settle over him just like had happened many years ago after John the Baptist baptized Jesus. Aware he was standing on holy ground this very hour, the normally talkative leader turned to the pastor and asked him to lead the group in consecration.

Pastor Ogwoka accepted the new challenge and immediately chronicled the events of the past week in one of the most heartfelt prayers this group of men had ever heard. He recounted the history of the great controversy and thanked God for placing him in His service at this final hour in the world's history. But just as he was about to say amen, a thunderous bang rattled the windows and the doors gave way. Seconds later, a woman's shrill voice was heard in the background. It said, "No, this is not the Armageddon, this is the end!"

Pastor Ogwoka ignored that voice and concluded his prayer. "In the name of Christ we pray—" And the elders said amen.

It was in that moment that the eyes of the pastors gathered here opened. No, not opened as in they stopped closing them; opened as in it was a revelation. They saw the world as the Luciferians had been able to see it. The world lay bare. It was decoded. They saw why the angel of the Lord had called out in Revelation with urgency:

> *Fear God and give Him glory because the hour of His judgment has come. Worship Him who made the heavens, the earth, the sea and the springs of water.*

✳

> *Fallen! Fallen is Babylon the Great!*
> *She has become a home for demons*
> *and a haunt for every evil spirit,*
> *a haunt for every unclean and detestable bird.*
> *For all nations have drunk*
> *the maddening wine of her adulteries.*
> *The kings of the earth committed adultery with her,*
> *and the merchants of the earth grew rich*
> *From her excessive luxuries.*

❋

Come out of her, my people,
so that you will not share in her sins,
so that you will not receive any of her
Plagues;
for her sins are piled up to heaven,
And God has remembered her crimes.

❋

Woe! Woe, O great city,
O Babylon, city of power!
In one hour your doom has come!

Indeed, this was not the Armageddon. This was the end!

TWENTY ONE

"**W**hat's up with you, Kate?"

Randy was now completely at a loss. For the past two hours Kate had just stood in the living room frozen. Her eyes had been glazed and her body stiff. But unlike a mummified, dead person, her temperature had remained rather high and her heart in a steady beat. No, she couldn't have been dead, Randy had somberly concluded, but she couldn't have been in a normal state either. How could a normal human being have gone two straight hours without noticeable breathing? And how could anybody have stood so still like a frozen robot awaiting command for its next act from its master?

But now Kate was back. Her return was just as sudden and as dramatic as her flight had been. No warning. No farce. Right there, as Randy thought the time had now come to call a doctor friend of his to look into this strange phenomenon that had taken control of his wife, Kate turned, looked at him and said, "Where are you going, sweetheart?"

The sound of her clear voice stopped Randy cold in his tracks. He looked at Kate as if she was a ghost or a miracle worker, then he edged closer cautiously. He glided his cheek right next to her nose to determine if she was breathing … and he quickly determined that indeed she was. Even her body temperature had returned to normal.

Kate said, "Randy, what's the matter with you?"

"Me? I should be asking you that question. You are the one who has been on the border zone since almost four hours ago. In fact, ever since we came back from Lee Funeral Home you've not been yourself. Has Vivian's death affected you that gravely?"

"It's not Vivian."

"Then what is it?"

Kate took Randy's hand and gave it a gentle squeeze. Aware what she was about to tell her husband would blow his mind away, she led him to the bedroom and asked him to sit on the bed, right next to her. Finally ready, she said, "A couple of hours ago you asked me if I'm a Luciferian, remember?"

Randy nodded guardedly.

"Let me tell you a story first—"

Over the next two hours, Kate told Randy the gripping story of her life. Yes, she was born into a pastor's family; and yes, she was a committed Christian, but that hadn't insulated her from the ferocious, focused attacks of the devil. Matter of fact, because of her pedigree the devil's agents had constantly locked her in their sights. They wanted to draw her in for two reasons: to discredit the pastor, and to use her to pull into Luciferianism other PKs—pastors' kids. Truth was…though she had lived a quiet life in school and now in Nairobi, she had actually accomplished a lot for the Luciferians. "I have been their most potent weapon in the fight to destroy ministers' families," she said.

"Really? But how?"

Her answer was oblique at best. "In the past two hours, I have learnt things I never knew about myself."

Randy drew a deep breath and shut his eyes. He knew this couldn't be good.

"Randy, two hours ago I was sent to the Synod."

"What!?"

"The Synod, of course, is where the Remnant Church has its regional headquarters. It's what we always call RCS."

"I know that!"

"Well, I was sent there to disrupt a meeting that's just ended."

"A meeting? What kind?"

"The church wants to fight back. The leaders of the Remnant Church have sensed—correctly, I might add—that the press will carry that story that played out at the Remnant Church in the morning. The leaders met at the Synod boardroom to figure out how to counter the negative press coverage they fear is inevitable."

"And you say you were sent to disrupt that meeting?"

"Yes."

"Who sent you?"

"The angel of light."

"Who?"

"The Great One."

"What in the world are you talki…."

"I was sent by Lucifer, don't you get it?"

Randy's jaw dropped. "Lucifer? The devil? So you are indeed a Luciferian?"

"It's true, Randy. Like I already told you, I've been a Luciferian since childhood. Unlike other Luciferian agents, though, I was assigned the easy task of corrupting the homes of pastors."

"But…but…but how?"

"Touch my neck."

Randy, fear on his face, lifted his hand and let Kate direct it to the spot where a black speck was planted nearly three decades ago. "This chip," she said after his hand found the exact spot, "has the ability to communicate with the soul of every human being—dead or alive. For the past thirty years, though, it was programmed to communicate with the souls of pastors' children and their wives. They were my assignment."

"What were you to do with them?"

"It's a long story, but this is basically how it worked. Whenever I come across a pastor's child or wife, the chip detects it. It turns me instantly into *agent mode* and transforms me into a sweet-talking angel. At a time like that, I draw the pastor's kid or wife into a conversation with only one intention—to corrupt the mind. My goal, when I'm in that state, is to make the PK or PW doubt the fairness and integrity of the mission. For instance—I ask them why, if God is for family, He lets Daddy be gone most days of the year. For the wife the approach is even more cunning and immediate. I ask them this—don't you have physical needs that have to be met while you're still young?"

Randy shook his head in total disbelief. "So all these years that I thought you merely had a split personality I was wrong?"

"Randy, I've been working for the Lord of the universe, the great Lucifer. He is the king of kings and lord of lords."

"Blasphemy," he snarled.

"The truth is difficult to take. I understand that."

"How about Vivian?"

"Her task was different," Kate said. "She was given sex."

"Sex? But how?"

"Randy, I only came to learn these things tonight, so don't think I've been hiding anything from you. But well, Vivian was given sex as her tool. Just an hour ago she showed me how she's used sex to crucify the souls of men and women. Viv has slept with hundreds of men and romanced hundreds of women. She has managed to turn sex into a social activity. Together with the many other agents similarly tasked around the world, Viv has worked hard to kill the conscience of TV, radio and magazine executives. She's made them believe that the raunchier a show becomes, the better the ratings it gets. Simple as that. In the end, though, going raunchy has served the Luciferian cause well. It has demystified sex; turned an activity God blessed and gave as a gift to married people into a game of ego, conquest and numbers. The point is—by taking glory out of sex, we have successfully put a dumper on marriage and turned the Garden of Eden story into a myth. Yes, it was we Luciferians who coined the phrase *Divorce is the future tense of marriage!*

"What many Christians don't realize is that once a man or a woman or a boy or a girl gets into the habit of sleeping around, he or she becomes a Luciferian and the number 666 is slapped on the forehead."

"666? The mark of the beast?"

"What beast? Why do you Christians call the angel of light a beast? The only beast I know is the tyrant of heaven who sent the angel of light down here because of a minor disagreement. Did He think He would bury Lucifer forever?"

"Kate, do you hear the words coming out of your mouth? Where did you meet Vivian anyway?"

"At the Synod."

"I thought she was dead?"

"Nope. Transformed."

"Into what?"

"Eternity."

Randy's tears formed. He was now scared and confused. "So that body we saw at Lee, whose was it?"

"What you saw was what we put in your mind. We wanted you to see Vivian so Vivian you saw. You know, when you saw Viv's body, the chic was actually already in Hong Kong on a mission."

"Are you saying Vivian is alive, Kate?"

"Randy, unlike Christians, Luciferians never die."

That was enough. Randy stormed off the bed and pulled out his cell phone. But just before he could dial, Kate slapped the phone away and snarled. Her eyes were red. "Don't ever tell anyone what I just told you—or you will die!"

Randy couldn't believe what was going on here. The first two secrets were at least bearable; this third one was just too much to take. Was there any more sense in living?

———

Over in Muthaiga, Carol and Jerome watched the scene playing out in Randy's home and laughed at the poor man. He looked so scared, so out of options. But after laughing, they got down to business and dialed Pastor Ogwoka's number. When the pastor answered, it was Jerome who talked. He said, "Pastor, I don't have to introduce myself anymore; you know the Luciferians well enough by now."

"I do. What do you want from me?" Pastor Ogwoka demanded.

"A meeting."

"A meeting? I see no need for one, Jerome. You and I serve different…"

"Tomorrow at 10.00 a.m., right in your office," Jerome said, cutting him off. "Make sure you avail yourself." *Click*.

Pastor Ogwoka hung up and dialed the executive director's cell number. When the tired leader answered, Pastor Ogwoka didn't waste time. "My elder, I'm not home yet, but I've just received a call from the Luciferians. They want a meeting at 10:00 a.m. in my office. Should we meet them or not?"

"Call back and tell them we are coming."

"I will," Pastor Ogwoka said.

"Have a good night now."

But the two men never had a good night. How could they when they knew they had just made an appointment with the principalities of darkness? Rather than sleep, they spent the night on their knees. The time for God to vindicate Himself had come. Was the church going to emerge victorious once and for all or were the determined, cunning Luciferians going to decisively defeat the church forever?

This was the apocalypse.

TWENTY TWO

Randy had tossed and turned the whole night. The troubled man had looked for answers in the annals of history, but had come by nothing so far. There was absolutely nothing to have indicated Kate's involvement with occultism. True as she had said, she indeed always got animated whenever she met pastors' children and wives, but that hadn't meant anything. Looking back now, he should have at least realized that her excitement hadn't been normal; she had been on a mission without even knowing it.

Now, however, it was too late. Given the way Kate had talked since Vivian's "death," she was too absorbed in Luciferianism to be rescued by him; he had to seek Pastor Ogwoka's help. Deciding not to wait till morning, he got off the bed at 1:30 a.m. and tiptoed to the living room. There, he flipped his cell phone and dialed.

Still in his study, Pastor Ogwoka looked at the Caller ID and wondered who it could be. The number was unfamiliar. Afraid it may be the Luciferians, he didn't answer.

Randy called again. This time, on a third ring, Pastor Ogwoka answered. "Hello?"

"Hello, Pastor. My name is Randy. I have a little problem I have to discuss with you."

"Now? It's 1:30, my son!"

"It can't wait."

"What is it?"

"It's my wife, Kate. She's an agent."

"Of?"

"The Luciferians. She's been since almost thirty years ago."

"And you are telling me this today because—?"

"Pastor, it's because her status as a Luciferian agent was just revealed to her this evening. She's been undercover!"

Over the next two hours, Randy filled the pastor in on what he knew. He talked about Carol, Jerome, Kate, the chip, the wealth, power and the bizarre interaction Kate always had with pastors' children and wives. He even talked about Kate's mission to the Synod. "Pastor, she warned I would die if I dared tell you what I've just told you!"

"She would kill her own husband?"

But before he could answer, Kate stormed into the living room and grabbed the cell phone. Holding it, she said, "Didn't I tell you not to divulge Luciferian secrets?"

"I had to talk to the pastor, Kate. I want him to help you get out of this mess."

"But he can't," Kate said. "My fate is sealed!"

Randy pursed Kate's words in his mind. *But he can't. My fate is sealed.* Didn't that sound like she was desperate for help? Hoping he was reading the situation right, he said, "Kate, if you want the Lord to deliver you from the powers of darkness, we have to see Pastor Ogwoka at once. The devil is not too powerful that the Lord can't deal with him."

"But they will kill me," Kate said.

"Wouldn't it be better to die in the Lord and await the second resurrection than die into eternal damnation?"

With forming tears, Kate nodded. And right then, out of the blue, Carol, Jerome and Vivian blew, like a pine breeze, into the living room. They looked like angels and were clad in long, white robes. But even in their "celestial" form, Randy recognized them and made a quick decision not to feel intimidated or afraid.

"You have a decision to make," Jerome said, looking Kate in the eye. "Will it be God or Lucifer?"

Randy moved in to protect Kate from the blood-thirsty trio in case Kate chose God. But as it turned out, tonight Randy's frail human efforts would not be needed. The one who locked the jaws of the lions to protect Daniel and reveled to John the Revelator on Patmos that He was the Alpha and the Omega was here.

Kate's hour of triumph had come!

TWENTY THREE

Sunday morning finally came. As usual, the area around the Synod was misty and wintry cold. Exercise-conscious folks were already jogging along the low-traffic road. For most Kenyans, this was just another fun Sunday, a day to fill the Pentecostal churches and Catholic churches across the land. The screaming headlines pasted on newspapers about the church and devil worship were just another church embroiled in shenanigans—nothing big. For the four leaders huddled at the Synod, however, this was going to be a decisive morning. It was going to be a macrocosm of the end of time. The apocalypse itself. But unlike last night, none of them was fearful this morning. The prayers they had offered individually, right into the wee hours, had reached the throne of grace and the Lord had allowed an outpouring of the Holy Spirit to fill their hearts.

The four leaders left the Synod at 7:30 a.m. in the Synod van. It was the executive secretary behind the wheels. The road that runs down the slopes of Kiambu, past the gate to the Synod offices, is paved and slopes into a fertile farm area that is only broken by the opulence of magnificent homes. Those farms and the trees that border their perimeter have a way of making it seem like the city is far out in the distance. But it is not long until a driver along this road lowers into the valley and takes that turn that suddenly rises into the beginnings of the city.

Using this road this morning, the four revived men drove into Westlands, then took Riverside Drive. The van rolled on safely, took a right on State House Crescent, then shot uphill. Within minutes, the leaders drove past the nation's executive mansion and took a left on Milimani Road. As they finally approached the gate that would usher them into the church campus, they kept quiet. It was like each of them was suddenly lost in private thoughts and final prayers before facing the devil. They knew it, felt it; realized that indeed this was bigger than Armageddon—it was the final battle for Christianity. A decisive win for the church this morning was going to deal a mortal blow to the forceful Luciferian agenda and open space for the Remnant Church to bring this world's history to a triumphant end. A church loss, on the other hand, would embolden the Luciferians and give them an opportunity to consolidate their gains and mount a final onslaught on the dispirited Christian movement—not only in Kenya, but worldwide.

Sensing the magnitude of this moment, the ancient deceiver, that great dragon, greeted the four elders with trouble right there at the parking lot. His ruthless agents bolted tight the van's doors, making them refuse to open, and blew sudden strong winds across the lot, almost tipping the church van. But the brave elders maintained their calm. They were not going to be intimidated by a loser who Christ defeated on Calvary many years ago.

In the middle of that parking lot commotion, Kate and Randy drove in and parked next to the van. Instantly realizing the danger the pastors were in, Kate jumped out of the car and called on the name of Jesus. The moment she did, the winds stopped and a lady's voice was heard in it. The voice came out in a fading fashion, as if the owner was in a panicked retreat. It said, *"Blessings unto you, Nairobi, for the Kingdom of the Luciferians has taken over this city. Great is he who sits on the throne of this world. Holy is Lucifer!"*

As soon as the voice went still, the van's doors opened and the four elders walked out. Then, together with Kate and

Randy, they went to Pastor Ogwoka's office. But the pastor was not in. Surprised he hadn't made it, the executive director dialed the pastor's number.

Pastor Ogwoka didn't answer.

The executive director dialed again.

No answer.

Fearing that something may have happened to the pastor, the four-man team got back into the van and were about to leave when the executive director's phone rang. He answered immediately.

"Hello, is that Pastor Ogwoka?"

"No. I'm calling on behalf of the pastor."

"Where is he?" the executive director demanded.

"Sir, we ordinarily don't do this, but the pastor insisted we call you right away. He is nursing serious injuries he sustained early this morning in an accident. This is the ICU— City Hospital."

"ICU? What's his condition? Can he talk?"

"He must rest."

"I'm on my way," the executive director said.

"I'll tell the patient." *Click.*

Half an hour later, the four men, trailed by Kate and Randy, got to the hospital where the Luciferians had arrived ahead of them and were already visiting with the weak pastor. Surprised to see them, Kate slowed down the team and warned them to be careful. It was while she still talked to the elders that Vivian—clad in a white robe—appeared out of the thin blue, just like last night, and said, "Kate, my dear, you have chosen to betray the Luciferians. You have failed our loyalty test. From this moment on, you must know that you are marked for death!"

"We all are," the executive director quipped. "But we will not die just yet, not unless the Lord allows it to happen." He walked toward Carol and Jerome, but when he got to the two, he first greeted Pastor Ogwoka, then he said, "Look, there will be no meeting between the principalities of darkness and the children of God. The one meeting that took place in heaven many years ago was sufficient. If Satan could not listen to God in that decisive moment in the history of the universe, why would he listen to us today? Don't you realize that because of that defiance this world has gone through pain and desperation and God was forced to put in place a plan of redemption?"

"Excuse me," Carol said indignantly. "We didn't call you here to listen to you; we called you to put you on notice. The days of the end have started. It won't be long until the Son of Man returns. It is our intention to welcome Him into a world controlled by the Luciferians. The great controversy that has raged on for years must now be concluded. Lucifer must take his place as the prince of holiness; the ruler of the universe; the great conqueror!"

Pastor Ogwoka, from his bed, said, "Lord, don't let them speak such blasphemous words this morning. Come down upon us. Give us victory over these forces of doom. Amen!"

In that moment, Carol, Jerome and Vivian dropped to the ground and frothed like they were possessed and were suddenly delirious. Christ was not gonna let the universe continue to wonder who was Lord. The hour of His vindication had come!

The End

Sam Okello is also the author of *Tears of a Nation*

DISCUSSION THEMES

A deeply controversial and informative work of this nature must be approached with soberness. The matters discussed in this book are critical for our salvation and must be tackled with seriousness. For those of you who have book clubs or youth groups or any other form of association and would like to invite me to explore the grave danger Christians around the world face today because of devil worship, call **0715596106** or write to **samokello@sahelpublishing.net**

The Questions:

- What does devil worship mean to you?
- Do you believe Christ has conquered devil worship and can set people free from this problem even today?
- Is wealth a tool in the hands of Luciferians as the author alleges?
- Would you rather have worldly wealth or Christ?
- What would you do if you suddenly discovered a friend is a devil worshiper?
- Are drug abusers devil worshipers?
- Is prostitution a trade controlled by the Luciferians?
- Do some pastors carry out themselves in ways that make them seem like devil worshipers?
- Is there any manner in which devil worship is fashionable?
- What is the connection between big business, politics and devil worship?

Friends,

The Lord has graciously blessed me with a creative mind for a time such as this. He has made it possible for me to create the world of evil within the framework of what we deal with today. It is my conviction that we can only defeat evil when we understand how satanic agents interact with our world on a day to day basis. But I suspect already that there will be those who after reading this book will entirely miss the warning carried through its pages and find it easier to label me and call me names…all in an effort to distract attention from this grave danger we face. My fear is that such folks will be playing right into the hands of the deceiver.

When you call me to discuss the issues raised in this book, I will be glad to tell you the wrenching story of the family whose little boy was deeply involved in Luciferianism. When this family told me about the agonizing nights of fear and defeat they had endured because of the boy's bizarre fondness of blood and occultist images, I asked if I could use their story to sound a warning to the larger global Christian family. The father graciously agreed. The mother vehemently declined. In the long run the boy's father and I decided this was too critical a matter to be swept under the carpet. And so *Decoded* has been written. It is my prayer that it will be used to bring glory to God by pulling back our children and youth from the tantalizing ways of the Luciferians, which in the long run lead to nothing but eternal damnation.

Sam Okello
Editor-in-Chief
Sahel Publishing Association
Nairobi, KENYA
Visit our website at: www.sahelpublishing.net

Other Great Books By
Sahel Publishing Association

1. *Cartoon Worship*, by Aunty Mary Clare Kidenda
2. *I Speak From The Grave*, by the late Dr. Julius Muchee
3. *Remember*, by Dr. Vincent Orinda
4. *Walking On The Edge,* by Joe Muchekehu
5. *Transformed To Transform*, by Peter Muya Hamisi
6. *Understanding Arthritis*, by Dr. Omondi Oyoo
7. *The Fate Of A Continent,* by Jimmy Anywar
8. *From My Heart,* by Counsillor Sam Wanyanga
9. *Tears of a Nation,* by Sam Okello
10. *The Bell Ringer: A Collection Of Short Stories,* by Collins Odhiambo

There will be many more books that will answer life's toughest questions for you, because as we always say, Sahel Publishing Association's promise is: Books that Speak To Your Hopes and Fears. Call us today: **0715.596.106 or 0731.651.927**. Talk to one of Africa's most-sought ghostwriters and editors, Hon Sam Okello, about your writing dreams!

Our website: www.sahelpublishing.net

We are in Kenya, the U.S.A., The U.K. and India

Publish your book with us today!

THE PRINCE KILLED THE DREAM ©

The dreams of a nation are receding fast,
As the Kenyan dream to a few now belong;
The lies of unity stand exposed, by the acts
Of appointments that kiss only Mumbi's big hut...

It once was a nation that stood like a vast ocean;
With possibilities that filled our hearts with joy;
Our children we knew would be great, even to
The moon and other planets they could go...

But now we look at the days gone by with heads bowed;
Bowed in shame for a jubilee that points to wasted
Years and the fear of a people who cling fiercely
To tribal glory and not the agenda of oneness...

We could have sent missionaries to the godless West,
But how can we when the goddess of Nairobi cries under
The rubble of Westgate, where she failed to stop
Big Kenya from killing Small Kenya?

The dream has into a nightmare turned, but dreamers
Of dreams never stop dreaming; that's why hope is kept
Alive, because once the prince is put in a cage
The new king will free Kenya to dream again...

By Sam Okello, in honor of the Westgate terror victims